T0065387

Shades of Endearment

Shades of Endearment

The most beautiful love story you

will ever read in a lifetime

Shahid Zuberi

Print information available on the last page.

Rev. date: 09/16/2020

To order additional copies of this book, contact:
Xlibris
UK TFN: 0800 0148620 (Toll Free inside the UK)
UK Local: 02036 956328 (+44 20 3695 6328 from outside the UK)
www.Xlibrispublishing.co.uk
Orders@Xlibrispublishing.co.uk
818767

CONTENTS

*Dedicated to my dear wife Rushda and
my children, Mona and Daniyal*

CHAPTER 1

The last two weeks have been hectic for Russell. A new computer system was launched, and he was at the helm of things. Downloading programs on computers, troubleshooting IT issues, fixing software glitches and answering questions all the time. He had to come on some Saturdays as well to do his work.

The system was up and running; it was a success; it was time to take a breather, he could relax.

"We need to get away this weekend, Emma." "What have you got in your mind?"

"I will take you to a place which will take your breath away," Russell said with excited anticipation.

"That would be nice." Emma's eyes gleamed.

Their lives were busy, real busy; Emma was working as a financial analyst in an investment bank. She had a distinguished academic background completing an MA in Economics and an MBA from London Metropolitan.

She was determined to scale the corporate ladder, and most of the time it was an obsession to the exclusion of all else.

Russell found this hard to live with such a rigid and obsessive outlook in pursuit of your dreams. He favoured a balance between hard work, ambition and life's little luxuries, little pleasures, such as having a carefree gathering of friends over a drink or going away for fishing, canoeing and hillwalking. He wanted to settle down and start a family. They met two years ago at a friend's party and forged a loving bond. They had so much in common and to outsiders they look like a perfect couple, well almost, nothing is perfect in this world.

Russell had a long weekend coming up and pleaded with Emma to take few days off either side of the weekend, and she agreed.

"We need to get away this weekend and stay in the woods, I want to be close to nature."

"Okay, where are we going?"

"I will take you to a place which will take your breath away." Russell had a twinkle in his eyes.

Russell often thought that time is slipping away from them and they should think about getting married starting a family and settle down. He was twenty- nine and Emma one year younger than him, and this was perhaps the golden time for them. Emma was not so sure, for her career was everything and in the cutthroat world of finance and investment banking she wanted to be the spearhead, always ahead of the game and she did not see motherhood as her priority; at least for now.

"We can always have children later; there is no hurry. People start their families in thirties and even forties. I am just far too occupied at present to think about start a family; this will put a hold to all that I have worked for."

"Think about it objectively Russell, do you want me to throw away all the hard work I have put in so far," Emma stressed her point.

"No one is asking you to leave; you will still be successful; there are ways to achieve our goals in professional and personal lives; people do this all the time. We can always seek help and advice, perhaps you could consider doing fewer hours for some time, and we can get home support, a nanny perhaps to help us at home and we'll be fine. Think about all the positives excitement and fulfillment this will bring to our lives."

"Motherhood is a lot of responsibility and to be honest, and this fills me with some dread."

It was nothing new; they had this conversation many times before, ending amicably with a silence where they both contemplated what has been said to each other.

They were no different to so many couples like them caught in the same dilemma. They loved each other dearly but were not able to reconcile their aspirations with the pace and direction of their lives.

~⌒◞

Tiverton Lake was an extremely picturesque long, narrow serpentine lake. It was roughly five miles long and less than a quarter of a mile at its widest part. The lake twisted and turned every few hundred yards and brought new panoramas into view as you glide on its surface. There were few small islands as well as nooks and crannies, making it extremely pretty. The lake was surrounded by mature woodlands of tall pine, alder, birch and willow trees along its banks. Densely forested areas were interspersed with clearing in the woods and sloped grassy banks that came down to the shores of the lake allowing canoeist and kayakers to stop, pull their boats on the bank, rest and picnic on the grass or just walk in the woods. The calm and secluded waters of the lakes attracted canoes and kayak lovers who were seen gliding on the surface of the lake in their boats. This serene and tranquil lake looked particularly stunning in summer. Azaleas, rhododendrons, hydrangeas grew in abundance around the lake and would almost hang in the lake at places. They would explode in colours of pink, purple reds and whites creating a magical treat for the senses. On quite windless days, the lake would turn into a virtual mirror reflecting flowers, trees and foliage in the crystal-clear waters. Fall season had its own charm as golden, beige, red and ochre leaves would fall on the surface of lake and reflections of the surrounding forest in majestic autumn bloom added a riot of colours.

Russell was fond of this place and had been here quite a few times with his canoe alone and with friends. There was a family pub at the north end of the lake called 'Chain and Boulder' with wide open decking area extending on to the lake with tables and chairs were laid out. On a sunny weekend, it was difficult to find a place, but Russell had made sure he has a reservation for a table. He also booked a log cabin for two of them.

Russell brought his canoe, ores and safety jackets. He launched the boat from the small decked pier at the southern end of the lake and they both got inside. Russell fixed the paddles in the ore locks; the canoe wobbled for a moment as Russell and Emma settled in their seats and Russell started rowing gently at first and then more steadily.

"Very pretty and photogenic, I am impressed," Emma said with genuine heartfelt admiration as she snapped several shots including Russell at the other end of the boat. She brought her phone out and took a snap of both of them in the frame.

"I would not use the phone on the lake," Russell said with a smile and Emma realised this, putting her phone back in her bag.

The canoe was gliding on the calm waters of the lake but its twists and turns meant a level of skill was required to keep the boat on course.

"You are paddling very well, can I help?" Emma asked.

"Yes sure, I will let you paddle later."

Panoramas changed as they canoed to about two miles and Russell spotted a gently sloping grassy bank on the right-hand side. He slowed the boat down and stepped outside and helped Emma get out and then pulled the canoe on the bank securely. They tied the boat.

"Good place to take a rest." "Yes." Emma nodded.

Russell lied down on the grass with his left leg resting on his bent right knee. Emma sat beside him.

"I love you so much." She leaned on his knee and said in a low voice.

"I know" Russell held her hand gently.

"I am not giving you the pleasure of having a family, sometimes I feel so bad about it," She said with some introspection.

"I can't help it; I am so confused." Emma looked up.

"Take your time and think about it, we are here to enjoy and get away from it all." Russell looked deep into her eyes and smiled.

The lay there in each other's arm for a while as sounds of birds and all kind of buzzing summer noises intensified around them.

Sun has come up and was bearing down on them now. The warmth of the sun was drying the grass and foliage around them fast.

"It's just so perfect."

"I knew you would love it."

They got up after forty-five minutes, pushed the canoe back into the lake and got in.

Emma wanted to row this time; the canoe wobbled for a time, and then Emma began to paddle steadily. Russell took over again after couple of miles, the lake was now bending left, then right like a river bend and was particularly pretty and photogenic and Emma captured some more shots in her camera.

They reached the north end of lake by noon, Russell pulled the canoe ashore, tied its rope to a post and secured it. They walked to the 'Chain and Boulder' and found their reserved table on the deck.

After lunch, they found their log cabin in the woods and spent the rest of the Saturday afternoon and Sunday exploring the woods walking, canoeing down the lake or just lazing around in the sun.

CHAPTER 2

They drove back home on Monday, the last day of their short break. It was a wonderful trip, and they felt reinvigorated but were no nearer to the solution to issue at the back of their minds.

After dinner, Emma said suddenly, "can we give each other time" and in a low voice added, "and some space."

"What do you mean exactly?" Russell sat up.

"Can we live apart for some time and see how we feel or perhaps how we feel about our future together." Emma was hesitant but serious.

Russell had a look of amazement on his face; Emma was the only serious girlfriend he ever had. He had pretty much made up his mind to settle down with her, marry her and have a family."

The atmosphere in the room turned sombre.

"I love you Russell, but I can't live with this burden of expectation every single day and that I am letting you down. I know it's me, darling."

"I know." Russell was lost for words for a moment. "There is no compulsion from my side, take as much time as you want to but not unlimited time; time does not stop for anyone." Russell was forthright, and his decisive tone surprised himself as well as Emma.

One week passed, it was a beautiful Saturday morning, light drizzle in the morning had cleared, and the sun has come out with blue skies and scattered white clouds.

Emma had wrestled with her thoughts all week. She had come to a conclusion; she summoned all her courage and had conveyed her feelings to Russell.

"I respect your decision, Emma, see what future holds for us, and remember I will always be there if you need me," Russell said with a heavy heart.

〜

On this beautiful Saturday in April 2005, Russell Morton and Emma Coleman, two attractive aspiring young, intelligent professionals, in love but undecided on the course of their lives decided on a 'pact'. A temporary separation for six months, to embark on a path of self- discovery and introspection and then meet again.

A gentlemanly pact, to reflect, ponder, explore and question themselves and do some soul searching. Nothing was written down, and they chose not to involve any of their friends as witnesses, it was strictly between them. There were no promises to get back together at all costs, no burden of guilt to carry, no apportioning of blame if life takes them to a different road.

"We will not question each other if our lives take an alternate path; will respect each other's decision."

Emma had said, and Russell agreed.

"No question asked and no answers given, unless we want to share willingly. If any of us wish to share our experiences, good or bad, they could do so, but there is to be no compulsion and no reciprocal expectations."
"Yep, accepted"

"We will only contact each other if it is a life or death situation."

"Interesting, agreed on this as well," Russell said with a wry smile.

The only promise they made to each other was to meet at the end of six months period, whatever happens, to reflect and exchange views.

The details were to be finalised in the next few days. Russell was to deal with things like ending tenancy early, cancelling services and settling the bills. The apartment was let furnished so there were no issues with moving, just personal belongings, clothes and other stuff, his canoe is easily tied to the roof of his car.

He gave four weeks' notice to his company; they were surprised at his decision.

"We are sorry to lose you, and you will be missed. The door is always open for you but good luck in your endeavours", his manager had said, and Russell felt better that his hard work and dedication was appreciated.

Emma was to keep her job but will move south; this will cut four miles off her commute to the city, which is a bonus. She had already made plans to share a flat with a university friend; who also worked in the city. Russell took a couple of weeks to complete formalities, settling bills, selling some of his items, taking back his deposit, those sorts of things.

There were few things he would not part with, a tapestry his mother gave him and hung in their living room, a carved walnut wooden box with inlaid flowers which he picked up from a car boot sale and always kept on his table.

Emma had gathered and packed her things neatly and had already made arrangements to move to a flat with her friend Debbie while Russell was completing all obligations for handover of apartment.

The day of parting was not easy for both of them but more so for Emma as she felt the burden of responsibility for this decision and very rightly so. Russell tried to make the situation a bit lighter with his jokes and gave all the impressions that this is indeed going to be a very short separation. He held her hands, kissed her and reassured her several times that he is always going to be there for her as they both moved around their apartment to collect their belongings. With each item of clothes books perfumes stationary 'bric-a-brac' being packed in the bags bringing the reality of their separation closer and closer to home. Russell hugged and kissed Emma one last time; she turned around before getting in her car waved goodbye and was gone. Russell noted dried tears on her cheeks.

He neatly packed his stuff in the car to maximise space. There were clothes, books picture frames, wedding photo of his parents, some free photos, old albums including his childhood picture album and other paraphernalia of life.

Bit by bit, all stuff was removed from the rooms, walls corners and corridors and once a vibrant, loving home was reduced to the status of an available apartment for rent. Russell wanted to get out of here. It was just a reminder that people make the home. As soon as you pack your belongings, remove pictures and your favourite paintings from the walls it starts to look alien to you, not yours anymore, and the overriding thoughts on your mind are to leave as soon as you can.

He packed his albums and photos carefully for the long journey ahead. They now begin to look outdated as digital photography was taking a firm hold, and all pictures are now stored on SD cards, CDs and computer's hard drives.

Russell remembered the day he got his first camera and the roll film and how carefully it has to be loaded. One mistake and the roll could be ruined before a shot was taken and sometimes ruined with all memories of an occasion on the film which was exposed incorrectly to light. He loved the meter showing how many shots are left on the film; all this is a thing of the past now. Russell took a deep breath as thoughts were racing through his mind. The relentless march of progress has brushed aside another fond memory of his.

Digital photography is so much easier and cheaper; still, it is difficult to forget the good old days; part of you is always left behind. When you move to a new system, a new way of working, part of you still linger on these memories, not allowing to let it go, memories, experiences call what you may, which makes us what we are today.

Russell smiled and packed his Yashica 135 in the bag. His philosophical musings had made him feel better. He reversed his car out of the car park and took a last look at the place and life he shared with Emma.

"Goodbye!" Russell mumbled not sure himself whether he was saying farewell to a place where he lived or to the life he so lovingly shared with Emma or perhaps both.

Russell wanted to visit his mother in East Anglia. He had called his mum a week earlier and informed her about the new developments in his life. His mother had met Emma and was very fond of her.

He drove on A1203 and then turned on A406 and joined M11 motorway north towards Norwich. It will take two hours, he thought.

This part of England always fascinated him, quaint, charming villages, flat but a calming landscape, The Fens, Norfolk Broads, Ely, Cambridge and the beautiful city of Norwich.

His mother lived in a small village between Norwich and Great Yarmouth. He spent three days with his mother, who was happy to see him as usual but a bit upset about their separation. Russell gave her many reassurances.

On Tuesday, May 01 2005 he headed north in his car. The IT industry was expanding rapidly over the last ten years since Windows 95 hit the scene and computers were firmly entrenched in everyday life. It was an excellent time to be an IT professional, and Russell knew this. He had applied for ten different positions in Midlands and up North. He was shortlisted for six and invited for interviews. He had made an itinerary to attend all interviews if possible. He would first go to Duxford, where a large engineering company was looking for an experienced IT professional to join their team. Russell had visited this place before and dreamed of coming here to live and work and this was his chance. He had also applied to positions in Sheffield, Leeds, Nottingham and Newcastle but he would like to be in Duxford if possible.

The city was surrounded by pleasant countryside with easy commutable distances to lakes, rivers and beaches. Peak District and Lake District were also within easy reach. Closeness to motorway to travel south and a boating lake nearby where he could take his canoe was other factors influencing his decision.

His interview went very well in Duxford. He went to interviews in five other companies in various towns and cities and was offered the positions in two places Duxford and Sheffield. He chose the job in Duxford and was happy with his decision. His company was situated on a purpose-built business park in a modern building with lovely views over the countryside.

He searched for rented accommodation for the next four days and settled on a first- floor apartment in a new development. There was a gym, a sports club and ample parking and a private garage for a charge where he could keep his canoe 'Tempest' and other stuff.

The apartment was within five miles of his workplace, just about perfect; he thought and paid the deposit to secure the place.

CHAPTER 3

It has been two weeks since Russell left and Emma moved away from Brentfield. Her new apartment was much nearer to her mother's home. Since they decided to separate to search for time and space to think it over, Emma wanted to be away from Brentfield to break away from the past and clear her head. She loved her job as a junior financial analyst in an investment bank, and there was the scope of her career progression, and she was well-liked at her workplace.

Her mother was living alone after her father died five years ago. Emma was able to slash at least four miles from her commute to the office each day and save valuable time. Her mother was saddened to hear of her separation, even if 'experimental' as Emma explained to her. She liked Russell and always reminded Emma that she is lucky to find a wonderful life partner in Russell. She tried to convince Emma but accepted her decision, albeit with a heavy heart.

Emma did not reveal all the finer details of the 'pact' she made with Russell. Her mother was fond of Russell and expressed many times that they will make a beautiful couple. Although saddened by their separation, she accepted the current situation.

"You are a fine young girl, and there is someone special out there for you, I am sure of this, and I so much hope it is Russell." Occasionally she would remind Emma on the brevity of woman's reproductive years and the relentless march of time. Emma never told her that this was perhaps the main reason she wanted to take time out of her relationship with Russell and think this over. On such occasions, Emma always nodded with a smile.

Emma was lucky to find her friend Debbie who also worked in the city in a different firm. She was looking for a female colleague to share the apartment with her. Debbie knew Russell in university years and had met him the year before when Russell and Emma were at a party of mutual friends. Emma did not hide anything from Debbie when deciding about her intention to share flat with her.

Russell's departure had left an empty void in her life, and it begins to hit home as she settled in her new dwelling. It was a lovely two-bed modern apartment with a kitchen diner and a spacious living room, situated on the first floor. There was ample parking on the ground.

She would get home by 6.30 pm, call her mother, check her progress and see if she needed anything, usual mother-daughter chit chat. Her mother was an active woman who attended regular dance and yoga classes nearby and looked after her health well. Debbie would arrive soon afterwards, and they exchanged the day's gossip as they had their dinner. They would have frequent plans to eat outside, go to a movie, theatre and attend social gatherings and Emma was back in touch with quite a few mutual friends through Debbie and Emma was grateful for this as her mind was distracted.

She would think about Russell almost every day, where would he be, what is he doing now, has she acted prematurely? Would she have given herself a bit more time, always realising that this was her aim to gain space and time with this 'experimental separation', Russell only agreed to her demands. Where did she go wrong? Has she been too obsessive about her career? Too self-absorbed, unable to see the bigger picture? The procession of thoughts would hit her whenever she was alone. Suddenly all the squabbles, all the difference of opinions and arguments appear to be dissolving in the mist of time.

She began to realise how accommodating, and understanding Russell was, but his nagging to start a family, slow down perhaps at the expense of her career was something Emma had significant issues with and this was the main reason for them drifting apart.

She would not go out of her way to meet anyone; if it happens it happens, I will allow fate to come to me. She is an attractive young woman; things can't be planned and pushed; she reassured herself. Doubts often resurface though.

What if she meets Russell after six months and he has a friend, perhaps much prettier than her and she would have nothing to show for her time apart from him. How would she feel, she would ask herself, this would be a devastating feeling for sure? The nagging doubts begin to raise their heads.

Sometimes she felt this to be a big mistake and knew she orchestrated this herself. She loved Russell and he was committed to her; we could have ironed out our differences, I should have made some compromises. At times she would come very close to fold all this up and give Russell a call and try to be together again. Sometimes she would feel she might meet someone more suited to her way of thinking, a driven and ambitious person like her, not laid back like Russell, who knows it can happen? But is this enough to have a similar way of thinking, will she ever get the same zeal and affection she got from Russell?

Thoughts and more thoughts.

She has a good job, meets people at work, at social gatherings through a mutual network of friends with Debbie. It could be tomorrow, next week, who knows at the local club, at swimming pool, in a party or at a conference. I would not go out of my way; I'm not desperate. I will not join a dating agency for sure; she reassured herself.

She was realising that relationship leaves an indelible mark, not easy to erase. Every day, every contact is like a brushstroke in a painting, always contributing to the overall effect, making its presence felt.

Painting was one pastime she enjoyed and had some natural inclination and talent. She inherited and perhaps influenced by her mother, who was an art teacher and an accomplished painter and continued to paint at this age. Emma did her first watercolour at twelve and won a prize in a local competition at thirteen years of age.

I will see if I could join a local art club to explore this hobby further, "it's a good idea" thinking about all the plans she drifted into sleep.

CHAPTER 4

One of Russell's colleagues Maggie was retiring after thirty years with the company. She was a pleasant lady with silver-grey hairs, a great and helpful colleague and always very nice to Russell. He was entrusted with the responsibility to get a bouquet of flower for her farewell party. In fact, he was the one who suggested this. He reached for the yellow pages and was looking for a local florist. A small advert caught his attention, '*Florarama*' fresh flowers bouquets with *Interflora* logo on the top left corner.

He conferred with a female colleague.

"Yes, it is a good place. I have been there once."

She gave him the directions on a piece of paper. He noted the phone number in case he got lost. He had recently acquired a new mobile phone, a smart, trendy flip screen phone with a camera. Russell still could not convince him whether picture quality of this would match with his Casio Exilim, his two-megapixel digital camera.

He drove for four miles, turning left at the traffic light, past petrol station and then further half a mile along the road.

There were three cottages side by side with neat white fences and tightly packed gardens with perineal flowers and few hanging baskets. Two homes had trellis with climbing yellow roses trying to get to the top. The sort of cottages you see on those chocolate tin boxes. A further fifty yards tucked away was the florist shop he was looking for. There was sufficient car parking for maybe six or seven cars, the flat ground was gravely, partly cobbled, and behind the shop he could see the lush farm fields.

Russell was pleasantly surprised to find a neat cluster of irregularly placed cottages and this lovely little florist place at the edge of town.

He was only twenty-nine but could remember his grandfather bemoaning the increasing order, industrialisation and commercialisation taking over each aspect of life. The character of towns and villages was changing fast. Geometrically placed homes, signs everywhere and mostly prohibitive, taking all romance and charm out of life. He could not agree more with his granddad. "Society needs rules, best use of resources and space; romance and charms are its collateral damage", he said to himself, but this place is quite pretty.

Rows of baskets were hanging from the florist cottage, and wonderful displays of fresh flowers were outside as well. He parked his car and approached the half- frosted glass front door. There was a wooden rectangular sign board above the door. The sign was old and rustic with peeling paint at the edges, on its grey background was sprawled 'Florarama' in yellow with maroon borders. As soon he opened the glass door, a couple of bells chimed announcing his arrival. The place was spacious and daylight was filtering through the glass windows. There was a broad counter about fifteen feet from the entrance. There were numerous shelves on either side, pedestals with displays of cut flowers bouquets of all sizes, dry flower arrangements and several bunches of seasonal flowers like daffodils, irises, tulips and roses were displayed in tubs, buckets and baskets of various descriptions. There were two alabaster sculptures on plinths on either side, one carrying a basket decorated with fresh flowers in her arm and the other carrying a vase with fresh flowers flowing out and hanging down.

Russell noted something unusual. There was a wooden frame supported on four pillars in the space between the front door and the counter, all the way to the ceiling. The columns supported a lattice of wood frame, like an indoor pergola, painted in subtle pink colour. With this frame were hanging, dozens of metallic bells of various sizes like in an oriental temple. The bells could be easily reached with the outstretched hand.

"Interesting", Russell mumbled.

There was subtle fragrance of flowers all around. The calmness and charm of the place has blown him away. He was about to press the bell on the front counter; suddenly, the side door swung open.

"Hello, how are you doing?", the lady said with a welcoming smile. Her voice had a shrill musical quality that sounded in tune with so many bells in the shop. "Yes, the person I am looking for." She was a smartly dressed woman of about fifty-two, wearing a white silk blouse and a floral skirt of muted pink colours.

"I am looking to get a bouquet for a colleague; it's a farewell party on her retirement."

"Sure, take a look around and let me know what you like. I have got a catalogue here for several bouquets for various occasions. I am sure we can find something for you."

Russell had no idea of buying a bouquet for such an occasion. He did not want to sound disinterested and had a good look around.

"Your place is lovely; I am very impressed."

"Thanks, I try to do my best, with a personal touch, of course" she added.

She opened a catalogue with laminated easy to turn pages in a binder and invited Russell to take a look. She was standing close to him, and Russell could notice a mesmerising fragrance off her.

"Do you make all these yourself?"

"Yes, most of them. I do have some help and some pre-made bouquets delivered as well. Arranging flowers is my hobby and now profession too." She said in her distinctive voice always smiling at the end.

She gave him some practical hints on selection of flowers and arrangements for this particular occasion.

He selected a large bouquet in a green vase with peach roses, purple freesias, pink limonium with leaves and foliage and placed the order. The bouquet looked good in the picture and the right size too, he was happy with his choice and her help. He got a printed receipt and a delivery time of about four days, 'just about perfect' Russell thought.

He asked her about the bells and chimes. She briskly walked to the wood frame and stood on her tiptoes to show Russell how to ring the bells. They were probably connected to each other with small colourless cords, Russell noted. She gave a slight tap on large bell in the corner, and this sent all bells ringing with some time-lapse as if an orchestra had come to life. The whole place buzzed with clattering of bells and chimes, their sound reverberating from every corner of '*Florarama*'.

"That's astonishing," he said as resonating sounds of the bells gradually died down.

He tried this time, and the bells sprang to life again.

"You have an amazing place; I would love to come back here; I mean just to be here."

"You are always welcome.

I am Pamela, Pamela Campbell, but you can call me Pam."

He shook her hand and noted her soft hands in his grasp and felt this a while longer with genuine admiration.

"I will come to collect the bouquet on Friday afternoon, and please give me your card phone number and opening times. She gave him the business card, and again her hand touched his hand.

"Goodbye for now, it's a pleasure to meet you and see your amazing place."

"I am Russell, just moved here four weeks ago from south. I am working in an engineering company as an IT consultant."

"So, pleased to meet you". Pam came to the door with him casually patting him on his left shoulder as she said goodbye.

Russell could feel her fragrance reaching him with such intensity which he never experienced before.

Russell was back at his desk, but he could not shake off the feeling he felt on this short trip to a florist shop on the edge of town called 'Florarama'.

The sheer magic of the place and Pam's enchanting smile, her fragrance was all around him. He thought long and hard about it, seemed a bit odd to him when seen with a rational thought process.

"Why am I feeling the way I am feeling, what was so special about this encounter", he mused to himself.

CHAPTER 5

'Fountainhead' was an impressive facility set in lovely mature gardens. It was established seventy years ago in a Victorian building then gradually expanded. The old building was incorporated tastefully in the large modern glass building and formed an impressive facade of 'Fountainhead'. There was an auditorium, playhouse, two cinema screens which showed contemporary films classics, art films and children's movies; there was an art gallery, a photography club and three restaurants. There was a pond at the front of the building and a sprouting fountain with statues from Greek mythology, the place took its name from this fountain perhaps. There was a vast car parking area behind the building. Several courses on art, drawing, photography, pottery, needle crafts, interior decoration and floral arrangements were available here for all skills level. The city was proud of this venue for its contribution to art culture and entertainment, and it was a thriving commercial venture at the same time. There was a gym with all modern machines and apparatus, and this required a separate membership.

Art classes at *'Fountainhead'* were a casual affair and this suited Emma. There was no syllabus, time frame or certificate at the end of course.

"It is pretty much flexible and depends on what you wish to get out of here." Art classes' organiser was a cheerful and gregarious woman, "I am Liz Danley; you can call me Liz."

"Hi, I'm Emma; this suit me just fine." Emma said, nodding approvingly.

"I work four days a week and would love to spend a couple of days here, perhaps Thursday and Saturday morning. In fact, I will be picking up paint and brushes after a gap of eight years." Emma said.

"You are not alone, dear; I see people coming back to art after much longer than that. Everyone learns and explores at their own pace; we just facilitate, guide, encourage you and provide an environment. I usually teach acrylic and watercolours; my colleague Brian is an expert in oils. We also have classes for designs and crafts, pottery, sculpture and floral arrangements and interior decoration. There is no pressure and no competition here, people with different levels of skill all work together and learn from each other as well."

Liz gave a good account of the place, and Emma loved this idea of learning and exploring in your own space and time with the help and guidance available. She believed that too much organisation, targets and time pressure stifles creativity. Liz took her for a walkabout the place. There was an open plan workplace with nooks and crannies created by work of arts themselves, statues and large indoor plants. Emma was impressed with its layout, "This is such a calming, inspiring place." There were numerous work stations, tables for drawing sketching, paintings, model making and crafts. Paintings stations and tables had sinks, washable work surfaces and ample storage for personal items and tools.

Emma chose a table and put her bag, sketchbook, watercolour sheet pad, watercolour tubes and an assortment of brushes and pencils. Several men, girls, young men, boys' women of all ages were busy in their work and trying to find a corner for themselves to express their creativity, their thoughts and aspirations. She noted there were two coffee lounges with comfortable seats and a kitchenette to make tea, coffee and drinks.

Emma started work on a landscape, after discussion with Liz. After spending two hours on her project, she was pretty much satisfied with the day's work; she was wrapping up things when Liz invited her for a cup of coffee.

"Come on, dear; make yourself comfortable here, would you like coffee or tea."

"Coffee, with milk and no sugar, thanks."

Emma noted a man sipping his coffee and looking at a sketch in his lap from time to time.

"This is Damien," Liz introduced him.

"Hi, I am Emma", she introduced herself with enthusiasm to the young man.

She sat across from Liz and the man, the artist, she knew now as Damien.

I am highly impressed with the facility, very calming and well organised and spacious. I love the idea of allowing people to work at their own pace, do what they like and support and guidance at hand. It's great, magnificent, more than my expectations." Emma was effusive in her heartfelt praise.

"That's very nice and satisfying that you liked the place and its goals and mission." Liz sipped her coffee.

"Indeed, I would enjoy my time here", Emma finished her coffee.

Liz excused herself after her drink.

Emma could note Damien was smiling all through the conversation.

"What interests you, watercolours, acrylic oils?" Damien asked.

"Mainly watercolours, I am picking up the brushes after eight years, what about you?" She asked Damien.

"I am doing some acrylic work on canvas, just like to paint landscapes, occasionally still life mainly flowers, vases and decorated flowers, bouquets, that sort of things" I am starting and have a lot to learn, painting gives me some peace and fulfillment." He said in a tone which carried a desire to soothe his inner strife.

"That's great, why not everyone should follow their dreams, their aspirations, there is as much time in life, and we have to pack a lot of things into this time. But I love the idea of working at your own pace, no deadlines, no classes and no competition."

"Yes, I agree, this place, I mean whole 'Fountainhead' is just a fabulous place." Damien nodded.

Emma noted he was well built but slim with chiselled features and deep intense blue eyes. His smile appeared restrained as if trying to overcome his inner strife, a deep sadness within.

"Nice to meet you, Damien, I will come here on Thursday afternoon and Saturday morning." Emma got up picked up her bag and other stuff, she shook his hand and in brief moment their gaze met. Emma could see his intense deep blue eyes much more closely, conveying a deep sense of melancholy in them. His grip was warm and firm.

"Nice meeting you, Emma", he raised his coffee cup and then she was gone.

CHAPTER 6

Emma felt at home in '*Fountainhead*' and its art classes. It was a welcome diversion from her pretty hectic week. She would immerse herself in the busy world of investment banking for the working week. Stock market variations, market trends, emerging markets, FTSE 100 index, currency fluctuations, graphs and figures, data analysis was the order of the day for her. She was good at it, contributing to the progress of her bank, that's what they are there, to make a profit. The work ethos were simple enough here, work hard, show awareness of market trends, the impact of world events, identify winning clues and combinations and back your hunches, take calculated risk and be rewarded for this. Emma knew this all and making her mark on the balance sheet of the company. Already there was talk of promoting her to a senior position.

Come Thursday; she would wind down, would change to a more casual dress and a relaxed appearance, a million mile from the corporate world image and go to Fountainhead. Debbie was surprised at her interest in '*Fountainhead*' and especially taking an interest in art again. She expected Emma to compensate for her hard work with indulging in parties, drinks, and social gatherings. She would still attend these happily with her office colleagues and whenever something interests her with Debbie and her circle of friends but would decline some requests if they clash with her attendance at *'Fountainhead'*.

Emma felt at home in *'Fountainhead'* and quickly made friends and was enjoying her time here. It was a pleasure to dabble with colours again. To lay washes on blank watercolour paper, see the colour bleed and merge into each other, painting blue skies, defining clouds horizons, trees, foliage was a joy again. She was perfecting wet in wet technique and had impressed her facilitators, especially Liz. She would occasionally break and sit in the north coffee lounge with glass panels all the way to the carpeted floor with a superb view of the garden and the iconic fountain in the courtyard. They were not allowed to bring drinks to their tables and work stations for a good reason. This allowed to meet up with other artists and hobbyists and exchanged thoughts. She would often stop by a friend's work in progress and was asked for her comments, critique. How do I merge horizon with the light blue misty sky still maintaining their individuality? My clouds do not look real at all; can you help? Should I erase these thick lines and blend colours a bit more? Those sorts of things. Emma would offer advice where she could.

Liz was seen rushing from table to table advising and helping artists on their quest to create something beautiful out of a watercolour paper, canvas or piece of cardboard. Sometimes giving them support and absorbing their frustrations when things don't turn out as they envisaged in the beginning, a common occurrence when someone is creating a work of art.

Emma was happy here, attending two sessions a week and so far, had managed acceptable sketches and landscapes. She noted Damien was working on a large canvas mounted on a board on an easel. It was a landscape but of a different kind. Emma could see a brown rocky mainly parched and craggy landscape. There was an intensity of purpose in his movements, his brushstrokes and he appeared absorbed in his work, Emma stopped by his station.

"You really have a talent for painting!" she complimented on his effort.

"Oh, thanks" he lifted his head from his canvas and looked at Emma.

"How long have you been painting?" Emma asked.

"About two years, since I left the army."

"You were in the army?" Emma said with a mixture of interest and wonderment.

"Yes, I was badly injured and was discharged from the army," he said in a low voice.

They moved to the coffee lounge and continued their conversation.

"I am sorry to hear this, were you serving abroad?"

"Yes, I was fighting a war."

"War" Emma repeated in a dreamy tone. "It was in Iraq, invasion of Basra in 2003." "Oh, I see, would love to hear your story."

Emma felt amazed at her own choice of words, a story for her maybe, a life and death situation for a soldier on the battlefield. She felt embarrassed and wanted to make amends for her words.

"It must be terrible; you hear so many harrowing tales of sacrifice, loss of life and injuries."

"Yeah" Damien nodded, "will talk about this some other time."

"Sure" Emma finished her coffee and realised she needs to return to her work.

Damien was an interesting man; he had several character traits, and now she knows he was a fighting soldier and saw active service in Iraq and was injured severely.

"Did she upset him?" she asked herself. She remembered it was he who broke the subject and volunteered the information, Emma rationalised and felt better.

Two days later, Emma walked in on a Saturday morning. She noted Damien, who was giving final touches to his painting. A sprawling landscape of barren craggy rocks interspersed with green desert foliage clinging to stones here and there.

"That has come on great, looks wonderful" Emma stopped by him.

"Thanks" Damien continued to apply stroke after stroke in darker section of his painting. Emma realised he is working with acrylic paints. "You like acrylic paints?"

"Yes, he nodded, oil is far too cumbersome for me, acrylics are best of both worlds."

"You should teach me painting with acrylics."

"Any time." Damien smiled.

You have that many brush strokes already and they have merged in beautifully. Emma praised his work.

"Yes, very much so every brush-stroke count, contributing to the final result, it just shows through even if you paint over it, just like our lives. Each day of our life leaves an impact even if we don't realise this". Damien was philosophical.

Emma shook her head in approval.

"I wanted to tell you about my experiences in combat, off course if you want to hear it."

"I would love to hear it as much as you want to tell me."

Emma knew sub-consciously it is related somehow to the desolation she noted in his deep blue eyes.

"I was worried I may have upset you, reminded you something, war is a terrible thing", Emma said with genuine empathy.

"Not at all, thanks for being so considerate speaking about my experiences is a form of catharsis; it always helps."

"We should meet out of here somewhere."

Damien said casually.

"Yes", Emma agreed.

As he moved back to his station, Emma noted for the first time he had a slight limp in his right leg

"He was injured in the war," she thought

For the next few days, Emma could not shrug off the thought of Damien from her mind.

What happened to him in the war, what were his injuries, how was he injured?

Does he have a family? Is he working? Unemployed? Is he carrying psychological scars from his past? Emma remembered his philosophical reference to brush strokes and how he said it the other day.

The thought of Russell crossed her mind, where would he be? How would he see her meeting up with Damien?

One thing was sure, she would meet him, somewhere else; allow him to get something off his chest.

CHAPTER 7

This was Friday, and Russell remembered he needed to pick up the bouquet. The farewell party was in the evening in a hotel around the corner from the company's head office. Russell pulled his car in front of *'Florarama'*. He opened the glass door to the welcoming chimes behind, the sounds of bells echoed from every corner of *'Florarama'*.

It was a bright sunny day. Russel had a sense of familiarity about the place this time around, the door chimes, the colourful displays of flowers, dry flower arrangements, statues carrying baskets of flowers and heavy bells hanging from the wooden pergola like in an oriental temple.

Roses, anemones, dahlias, cyclamens, carnations, cala lilies, asclepiad, pink yellow and orange germini flowers, carnation, gerbera, antirrhinum, pittosporum and white oriental lilies were all there in various arrangements in raised vases on pedestals; a fresh, subtle fragrance was pervading the place.

Russell took a short stroll through the place waving to Pam, who was serving customer at the counter. She waved back with a smile "will be with you shortly", her voice reverberated just like the door chimes or Russell felt it that way, he was not sure. Her voice has this quality of lighting up a place.

The woman at the counter gathered her flower bouquet thanked Pam as she came after her to keep the door opened for her. She turned back nimbly as If walking on water. She was full of smiles "your bouquet is ready" she went to the side room and came back with a most beautiful vase of fresh flowers complete with panicum grass and salal leaves.

"That's just amazing, truly beautiful" Russell gave a good look at the bouquet, he was lost for words.

"I am glad you liked it; hopefully this will be a befitting present for someone leaving." Pam gave a final glance as she turned around the bouquet in its vase to see everything is perfect and then gave some tips to Russell on how to keep it in top shape until presented. Russell could feel her fragrance over the top of cut flowers in the bouquet, and he gave her a look, an admiring look. She was wearing a white skirt with buttons right down to the bottom and a beige brown blouse with thin floral pattern on it, she had a necklace of light brown beads and earrings to match.

"You are looking so pretty, so elegant," Russell said with a lot of affection and utter conviction and Pam was taken aback with his boldness and Russell could see she blushed a little.

"Your place is so magical, and you are an amazing person" Russell was effusive in his praise.

"Oh thanks, that's very kind" Pam chuckled.

"Can I come here again?"

"Of course, you can, it will be a pleasure, feel free to drop in any time, to look around have a chat perhaps."

"I wish I were working here," Russell was looking for a good enough reason sub-consciously to visit her.

"You could help me with floral arrangements."

"Really" Russell sighed "I would love to."

She continued to wrap the bouquet in final layers of special paper and then handed over to Russell. She walked in front of him, opening the door for him and smiled as doorbells chimed again. Russell passed almost brushing her arm as he took the huge bouquet out of the door and felt her fragrance permeating his whole self. She came to his car to see he tucks in the vase properly in his car for safe transit.

Russell put his sunglasses on, reversed the car and waved goodbye to her and drove off.

CHAPTER 8

Russell was settling fine in his new job, and it was almost six weeks since he left Brentfiled in south to move up here.

He thought of Emma that night. How will she be, did she meet anyone? Does she remember me or think about me?

On one occasion he came so close to calling her, nearly.

Russell thought many times to go to *'Florarama* 'but could not do it. How would it feel, there was no reasonable pretext to this?

He can't go for another bouquet from the shop; it will look odd and almost surely tell if he makes an excuse to buy. He knows his eyes will betray the truth; no, he can't do that.

Russell was wrestling with his thoughts for ten days since he picked up his bouquet, which was a smash hit at the office party. Wednesday was his off day usually reserved for his shopping, mundane chores like cleaning, kitchen and so on.

Russell drove to *'Florarama'* on Wednesday, dressed in blue jeans and casual beige cotton shirt; he parked his car and stepped outside. It was about 11.30 am. He opened the glass door. The clanging of metal chimes reverberated in the whole building. The counter was empty, Russell hesitated for a moment. Pam emerged from the back door.

"Come on in" she was no less melodic than the chimes themselves. Come in the back room."

She said with so much certainty as if expecting him at this time for something.

"I am unpacking some boxes and arranging some bouquets." Pam led him to the back room.

Russell noted neatness and order everywhere he looked. There were cabinets and drawers on two sides like a modern kitchen and a large central island with a shiny black worktop surface.

There were several cardboard boxes laid out in the corner. There were vases of all descriptions, containers, wrapping papers, ribbons, and all sorts of pliers, cutters, secateurs staplers and knives and so on.

"Take a seat, dear." She said with her usual affection.

Russell settled on a neat white bar stool. She continued her work while speaking to Russell, never allowing a moment of awkwardness to creep in and he was so thankful to her.

He always found starting conversations difficult.

"You look different", she said with some admiration

"Yes"

"This is my off day", Russell said, remembering he came in more formal clothing last time.

"I thought I should say hello to you."

Russell could not think of anything else.

"That's very kind of you." Pam smiled.

"I hope I am not interrupting your work."

"Not for a moment, in fact, delighted to see you." Her distinctive melodic voice echoing in *'Florarama'*.

The conversations were interrupted with door chimes ringing as a customer approached the counter.

"Excuse me."

She went past the swinging door, and he could hear her jingling voice interspersed with that of the visitor. She was back again after a while.

"Would you like a tea or coffee?"

"Coffee would be nice", Russell nodded.

She opened a cabinet and pulled out two cups with saucers; he noted her refined taste reflected in everything around her. She turned the kettle on.

"It's so peaceful here."

Russell looked around the place.

"You looked so fresh, rested." Pam looked at him

"Oh, thanks."

"So, tell me about yourself." Pam was now pouring coffee for him.

"I am from down south, Brentfiled, just moved up here six weeks ago, working as an IT expert in a large engineering company.

I am actually from Norwich; my mother still lives there."

Russell felt a pang of guilt as he did not mention Emma as part of his life. How life was different just two months ago, he thought.

"It is a nice place to live; I like it up here."

"I am so pleased you are happy here; indeed, it is a lovely place to live." Pam said with some assurance.

"Can I help you with something?"

Russell thought this was good to have a friendly chat beyond introductions.

"Sure, I was opening some boxes, you can help with these."

She was moving in her '*Florarama*' like a wide wing butterfly with ease, grace and eager restlessness as if gliding through the air.

Russell noted an elegant charm about her movements; moving boxes, opening drawers, washing pots and wrapping papers or tying ribbons all done with effortless ease.

"How long you have been doing this?"

"About ten years now," she said while clipping branches of foliage to fit in a vase.

"Since my son left school to go to university, he works in the oil industry, sometimes offshore."

"A mother," Russell thought, her children would be so lucky to have such a lovely devoted mother, he thought.

What about her husband, does she have a partner? But realised no details of this forthcoming and did not want to probe this either.

He was ever so aware of his position in life. The thought of Emma sprung up in his head, where will she be at this time? what is she doing, how will he describe his current relationship status, single, separated? uncertain?

Not easy to describe. In the office, Russell appeared a single and a desirable young person. This was a different place; the sort of intimacy he felt here with Pam was enough to convince him that they will meet again.

"Would you like to help me to unpack those boxes?"

Pam pointed to the cardboard boxes in the corner.

"Yes, sure" Russell came back from his wandering thoughts.

He was relieved that conversation has moved on to here and now and not lingering on something he was not ready to talk about at present.

She gave him a cutting blade and showed him where and how to open the boxes.

He opened the first box, extra careful. The box was full of cut flowers neatly wrapped in delicate wrapping papers.

They had long strong stem and tightly packed double whorls of petals with a central dark centre.

"That's germania; quite robust flowers come in twelve different shades." Pam introduced him to flowers as he worked.

Russell carefully put the flowers in vases on the black work surface in the centre.

Opened the second box, giant white lilies, another box had thin decorative fern-like foliage, delicate leaves, and some ornamental grasses.

"That is pistache and panicum grass, 'salal' leaves and 'thlaspi green bell.'

They are all used to make the bouquets."

Russell realised there is so much go into a bouquet to make it worthwhile, something adorable and how little attention he had paid in the past to something like a 'flower bouquet'.

"I did a course on floral arrangements," she said reminiscing about the moment that changed her life with immense fondness and satisfaction.

"Something just clicked; I decided there and then that I want to be a florist.

I started from home first, and then this place came up, and I moved here about eight years ago.

We get chrysanthemums, roses, lilies, oriental lilies, sunflowers, pittosporums, asclepias, alstroemeria, carnations and many more.

I do all the floral arrangements myself; the shop will close to the public today at lunchtime, and I will work here until evening to finish all the bouquets."

"That's a lot of work."

"Oh, I love my work." She smiled, turning towards him.

"So, impressed with your passion and dedication for what you do." said Russell.

"The look on people's faces, when they pick up their flowers, a big payback for me.

All manners of human emotions, celebrations, house warming, sharing grief, mourning, weddings, birthdays, and anniversaries all expressed with flowers. It's like a blank canvas, and I add layers and layers of flowers and leaves, just like days and moments in life, every petal count in the final reckoning."

During all these musings Russell noted she hardly stopped for a moment. Picking up flowers, cutting them neatly, removing dead leaves, adding layers as she said and cleaning at the same time as she went along. She would occasionally ask Russell to pick up a shear, a scissor, plastic wrappers, ribbons, move vases or unpack packets of plant and flower foods.

Russell, the IT expert, the carefree young twenty-nine years old from the south in search of self-discovery, had unwittingly became an assistant in just one morning in a little place called 'Florarama', and strangely he felt good about it.

In between, she would go to the front desk and serve a customer and come back through the swinging half doors.

Finally, she said, "time to close the front door," swung the open sign to close and locked the front door and came back to where Russell was standing trying to cut open the last box.

"They are chrysanthemums, used for anniversary weddings, and many more occasions. They are white lilies, also white roses there used in sympathy flower bouquets."

"Happiness and grief do a slow waltz in the front garden of life." Pam said looking in the distance.

"Slow waltz of happiness and grief, I will remember that, brilliant expression," Russell repeated in a dreamy tone.

Russell touched her hands many times when helping with her work and noted her hands to be extra soft for someone working so hard. You can't explain everything, he thought to himself. Few things are better left there, unexplained.

Russell was enchanted by her demeanour, her sweet voice and her flowing movements and her unique fragrance emanating from her more like oozing from her, he thought, and this was drawing him ever closer to her.

"I should be going now," Russell looked at his watch.

"I will close the place for two hours and then work in the afternoon to complete all the bouquets, next morning you will see them in shelves displayed on front ready to be picked up."

She came out with Russell, looked the front door and got into her red hatchback.

The sunshine was now pervading this little corner of town, and there was freshness in the air. Pam put on her dark goggles and lowered the driver side window.

"I will invite you to come for tea at my place then we can talk perhaps instead of making bouquets." She smiled at Russell.

"Yes, that would be nice. You have a lovely place; I enjoyed coming here immensely and helping you." The sense of familiarity and a bond of affection developing so naturally between them surprised him.

"That's very kind; you made my work so much easier." She settled in the driving seat and waved goodbye to him. Russell heard her engine start and her reverse gear engage and waved goodbye to her.

He put on his sunglasses and backed his car and drove off. He was still reliving the incredible morning he had in a beautiful little place called 'Florarama' as he drove home.

CHAPTER 9

Pam had invited Russell on a couple of occasions to come to her home for coffee. He felt her spontaneity and warmth made him so welcome. He was flattered but did not want to go immediately. He phoned Pam and checked if a Wednesday afternoon is fine, which she indicated is possibly the best time when she finishes work early and this was his off day as well.

He drove to her home, a neat bungalow on the outskirts of town. This was a leafy suburb and quite pleasant. Her car was in the driveway, he parked his car next to hers on the gravelled area. The driveway was screened with a row of tall cypress trees, and he felt somewhat better. Russell was about to ring the bell, but Pam opened the door and said, "come on in." Her voice was reverberating in the whole house just like the jingling chimes in *'Florarama'*. She was looking fresh graceful and elegant, and there was a shiny radiance about her. Her light ash blonde hairs were neatly curled. She wore a light pink skirt of medium length and a silken transparent blouse accentuating her bosom encased in a firm white silky bra which was only subtly visible from a distance.

"You are looking so pretty, so elegant." Russell complimented her with a smile.

"Oh thanks." Pam was all smiles

She gave a good laugh and hugged him and then kissed his cheek lightly. He had his arms around her and felt her softness against his chest and wanted this embrace to never end. Russell could feel her fragrance engulfing him, coming all over him, a drizzle of euphoria was all over him again.

He sat down on the beige colour sofa and looked around the room. Everything about the place exuded class, the room was subtle not overly decorated but had a feel of neatness and uncomplicated approach she had towards life. There was deep blue carpet on the floor with sparse floral motifs; a large bay window had few decoration pieces not obscuring the vision out of the window.

There was a William Turner's painting on the wall depicting a rural Suffolk scene, probably 'Flatford Mill', he thought. There were off white curtains neatly tied back on either side and afternoon light was filtering through into the living room in abundance.

Russell noted a framed picture of Pam with her son with his graduation gown and cap. There were some framed pictures of colourful birds in a cluster.

"Lovely home, very nice, it's so peaceful here." Russell said after taking a good look.

"Thanks, you liked this; how are you settling in then."

"Yes, very well, the company is brilliant and all colleagues and staff are fantastic, excellent ethos and working environment. I am so lucky to be working here and finding a job so soon."

"Tell me about yourself, your life, and where were you before."
Pam asked

"I was born in Norwich and lived there with parents; mum still lives there. I have one sister who lives in Australia now, married. Russell was taking his time.

"Went to school there and then university, London Metropolitan, did master's in computer science there. I play rugby, table tennis and also badminton, love to watch football, cricket and tennis. I always loved the water and spent my childhood near lakes ponds and marina; my father was secretary of local boating club. I love sailing, canoeing, kayaking. I have a canoe which I have named 'tempest'; I take it to lakes, rivers and canals whenever I can and if time permits."

"That's very interesting, you are an outdoor person, I love to walk and go out as much as I can, feel the fresh air changing seasons, it is a blessing to have so many lovely places to visit at such short distances."

"I was working in Brentfiled just outside M25 in an IT company. I lived nearby about ten miles commute, with Emma." Russell continued his life journey.

Pam was listening attentively, and her smiles gestures and nods reassured Russell that she is interested to hear about his life so far.

He continued, "We met at university first, have known her for six years and were living together, we had a rented apartment not far from my workplace. We were there until two months ago.

"She is a delightful girl, I loved her and wanted to marry, start a family," Russell said in a low voice.

Russell looked at her and found her very attentive.

"Emma is very driven, very ambitious. She has masters in economics and an MBA and is working as a financial analyst in an investment bank and her prospects are very bright.

We had some disagreement lately, starting from my desire to start a family, keep a balance between living life and working.

Emma does not see things this way, for her its success at all cost even personal cost. I never forced her, but my priorities are different, and this thing came between us and we kind of begin to drift apart.

I am all for working hard, getting ahead in life, be competitive, but I value life and the passing time and wish to keep a healthy work-life balance and that's no too much to ask for.

She thought motherhood and family would stand in the way of her career at least for the next few years.

My expectations were bearing down on her. I never forced Emma though, no shouting, no arguments; it was calm and civil between us. I just made her aware that time is slipping away, I am going to be thirty next year, and she is one year younger than me."

Pam took a deep breath, deep down, she admired his honesty; he bared his soul to her without putting any blame on Emma but putting in words a life situation as it happened.

"Is she in contact with you? coming to see you here." Pam said with empathy.

"No, we made a pact, in a very civil sort of way, to move away from each other for six months. As Emma puts it, to go on a journey of self-discovery, give each other time and space. If life leads us to a different path, so be it. There is no burden of guilt, nothing to explain to each other. We will not contact each other during these six months unless it is a life and death situation.

We made a firm promise, though, that we will meet after six months to see how we changed and how our perspective on life changed and towards each other and to see if we wish to be together again.

I could have stayed in the same place, found another job but I wanted to get away from it all. That's why I packed my bags and hit the road to see where life takes me. I was literally on the road with no firm plans."

"I see that's how you come to be here in Duxford." Pam could feel his inner strife and struggles as Russell narrated his flight north in search of meaning to his life.

"Indeed, I applied to several positions and got this job; dream run really in an increasingly competitive world. I am incredibly lucky to find a good job so soon."

Pam felt so much sympathy for him and felt like go and sit next to him, hold him, hug him and comfort him. She did not wish to break his flow of thoughts. It was apparent that she is the first person he is sharing all this since leaving Emma.

"Is she still in the same place?"

"Emma values her job immensely. She has moved to another town in the south and commutes from there. She is sharing a flat with a friend whom I know as well; she also works in the city.

I think this is the best we could do in these circumstances, and it will help to clear our minds, see things in perspective and see whether we change as persons, how it impacts our lives and take it from there.

There are no firm promises to get back together and we will respect each other's decision if we want to go our separate ways." Russell lifted his gaze to look in Pam's eyes.

"So, that made you come here, it's a lovely place; I like it here and have been here for fifteen years now."

Pam was moved by his words, deeply impressed by his honesty and how he used 'we and us ' rather than me and I.

"Thanks ever so much for sharing this all with me; you are so open and honest."

"Thanks for listening; you are the first person I have confided with my journey."

"Would you like a cup of tea or coffee?" Pam asked with her typical, jingling voice full of affection.

"Coffee would be nice."

Russell followed her to the kitchen and started helping her. Cups, milk from the fridge, the sort of help men usually offer.

Pam asked him to get two bone china cups and the milk as she set up the coffee maker and switched it on. She set up a tray with some biscuits on a plate and brought this to the living room. She asked Russell to pull a side table to centre and placed the tray; Russell added some milk for himself and asked her.

"Just a little"

"You make wonderful coffee; this would be an excuse for me to come here more often." Russell was jovial.

"Yes anytime, it is so nice to have you here."

"Now tell me about you, the beautiful, elegant and charming florist." Russell was effusive in his praise of her as he leaned forward on the sofa to give all his attention.

"Me" Pam's eyes gleamed and she started after a pause.

"I was brought up here in the North; I have one brother who lives in Cumbria. I first went into nursing, then worked as a medical secretary for twelve years in a local hospital.

I was married at twenty-three, had Peter one year later, my son, you see him in the picture, lovely boy." She pointed to the framed photo on the wall.

Russell turned his head to look at the picture for the second time showing admiration with his gestures and look.

"Then I got divorced," she said plainly without any emotions or bitterness.

Russell put his cup on the table and sat forward.

"Why! how can this happen? How can someone divorce a beautiful, kind-hearted, charming and elegant woman like you?"

"Yes, it happened. My husband liked someone else and then announced he is leaving me.

Peter was only about ten at the time, in school. I continued working to support my son and the home."

Russell tried to visualise the profile of a man who was blessed with the most kind, beautiful and elegant woman, a hard-working devoted mother, and he chose to leave her.

He felt anger at the man and realised this had happened so many years ago.

"I didn't want to stir bad memories, but if your husband was around, you would have so much support.

I mean this must have been hard for you to keep your home, bring up your son and then venturing into a new business."

"Everything happens for a reason. Sometimes hardship brings the best out in people. I take one day at a time; I don't think or plan too much ahead.

About eight years ago, I attended a course with a friend for flower arrangements and floral decoration and dry flower arrangements, that was something, and I was hooked.

You don't know what virtues and capabilities are dormant within you until the right time comes, and sometimes you surprise yourself, something similar happened to me.

I started work from home at first; it just went from there. This place came up for sale, and I transformed into *'Florarama'* you see today. However, I do get help from friends sometimes which is great." Pam said with her usual smile.

"Brilliant, excellent, your hobby and vocation just suit you so well; complement your soul, your nature. I would have great difficulty visualising you in the role of a secretary or nurse for that matter. I am sure you must have been excellent in those roles too. I still could not comprehend how someone could leave a sweet woman, sweet and beautiful in every sense of the word, I mean it." Russell's face flushed.

Pam smiled, feeling the force of his emotions, "I know you mean it and I could see this in your eyes; you are so honest about everything, you keep your thoughts so simple, will help you a lot in life."

Russell had finished his coffee and felt an intense desire to hold her in his arms to kiss her, to hug her. He was sat across from her in a well-lit room with a large bay window; people could see him. He did not want her integrity to be questioned. Pam was pretty casual about his visit to her home though, but he was pleased to have his car parked securely behind tall cypress trees hidden from public view. An intense bond of affection gently crept in and got hold of them on this quiet afternoon, and they both felt it. They appear to know each other for a long time.

"How are your neighbours?" Russell changed the subject.

"They are fine; Sam lives next door, a widower, very active does a lot of walking and gardening. Geoffrey and Margaret live on this side, nice people. Margaret had not been so well lately. I help them with shopping, hospital visits whenever I can; their children visit from down south sometimes.

There is a young family across the road, two lovely children I like them lots."

Russell noted how she picks all the good things in others, not a shade of negativity or doubt. Is she just lucky, or does she make the best out of the world around her?

Russell thought, what about her husband. The only man she loved had a son with him, what about him. She married a man who could not value her, could not see her inner beauty, her energetic, loving and tender soul ready to shower her affections on the next person she meets?

He felt he is despising the man who left a gem of a woman in the middle to bring a child on her own and here she is with no bitterness, no negativity towards life or him and no self-pity.

She has chosen the right hobby and right vocation to channel her positive energy to devote to flowers, bring happiness, lessen and dilute grief in the world around her.

Russell often wondered about some calm and satisfied people in this vast sea of humanity and often thought of their approach to life; what makes them so calm composed and optimistic and cheerful? In the maddening rush of life around us, we do come across some human beings living at their own pace, not flustered by chaos and pressures around them.

Russell was fond of Thomas Gray's elegy, his favourite verses came to his mind.

Far from the madding crowd's ignoble strife
Their sober wishes never learned to stray;
Along the cool sequestered vale of life
They kept the noiseless tenor of their way.

"What are you thinking?" Pam saw him lost in thoughts.

"Oh yes, thinking about Thomas Gray's elegy and how this fits your persona, your life is so calm and serene in this chaotic world." He told her about the lines of the 'Elegy', and she gave a good laugh.

"So, you like my cool sequestered vale". Pam smiled, and Russell looked at her beaming face. He felt an intense desire to hold and hug her but said in a jovial tone without betraying his ardent affection for her.

"Indeed, I do."

"Shall we go out for a walk?" Russell thought he had been sitting for some time but did not wish to leave her company.

"Yes, where do you want to go."

"I had seen a lovely walk along a river when I was exploring this area; it is along the River Ure."

"I know where you mean."

Russell offered to take her in his car but realised this should be her choice.

"You can come in my car, and I will drop you off at home, or we can go in your car, or we can take our cars separately, whatever you like and suit you best."

"I will take you in my car, I know where it is." Pam picked up her keys.

Russell got his camera and jacket from his car, Pam drove down A26, then a right turn after five miles and then a left down a country lane, and they reached a gravelled car park. They got their jackets out and set off on the path along the river.

River Ure was a navigable river eventually joining the Union canal and had several picturesque bridges along the way.

Scores of boats were moored on the side of the footpath. Some were covered with waterproof covers; some were empty and in some people were pottering about. Russell had a fascination with boats and water ever since he was a child. He loved seeing people spend hours in their boats doing little things, cleaning, polishing repairing, mending or just reading a book. It is their way of spending time where they are most comfortable. Some boats were returning from their trips.

Pam was impressed with his power of observations for finer details which people in this busy world either take for granted or just don't see them as important.

The sun has come out again, making the sky a deep blue colour with some fluffy clouds, and it felt warmer. Russell had taken off his jacket in his hand.

"So, what is it you do here in your firm?"

"I work as a computer expert, more appropriately, an IT professional. The IT sector has expanded exponentially in the last ten years." Russell told her.

"I make sure that computer programs are running smoothly, download and install new programs, debug programs, fix IT issues on a day to day basis, teach people how to use computers efficiently, prevent virus attacks, and remove viruses, that sort of things."

Again, Pam was impressed with his intelligence and eloquence using few words to tell a lot.

"Perhaps you could teach me few things, I can only receive and reply to emails."

Pam laughed.

"It will help your business, set up a website, put all your lovely floral arrangement and bouquets online, and people can place their order on your website."

Pam gave an incredulous look, and Russell realised this is too far-fetched for her at present.

She is in control and happy, and that's what matters, he regretted his words.

"That's for future, and if you really wanted this." He sorts of wanted to make amends for his transgression.

"Yes, I know most people who come to my place. I make new friends all the time, and prefer it this way."

"Your personal touch makes this so much more beautiful for people you deal with."

Russell realised the same dilemma he had been grappling with, in his own life, success vs happiness, how do you balance the two in an increasingly competitive world. By and large success and material gains has become the yardstick of happiness, and it should not be this way. He saw this lovely florist in a small city balance this beautifully without reading books or articles on the subject. Russell nodded meaningfully.

They have walked for about a mile, and the river begins to widen here and turns to join the union canal eventually. The sun was getting low on the horizon, creating an orange glow; perfect light conditions as they began their walk back along the path. Russell took some great shots of boats bobbing on the water. He included Pam in a couple of shots. She smiled and obliged. Russell noted that she has this lovely way of standing with one leg slightly behind the other, giving a subtle side on pose for photograph.

Pam drove back home and asked Russell if he would like another cup of coffee. Russell sat for a couple of minutes in the living room, collecting his thoughts on this beautiful evening he had with Pam.

"Some other time, thanks ever so much for a lovely afternoon, brilliant coffee and incredible evening walk. I would always cherish this. Russell hugged her tightly and kissed her on her cheeks and then another hug this time longer as if he did not want to let her go. He could feel all of her softness fill his arms so effortlessly rubbing all her affections on him. He was in a drizzle of euphoria almost drowning him.

He said goodbye and drove out of the drive, as he turned the corner at the end of her close, he could see her silhouette in the big bay window.

CHAPTER 10

Damien was born in Kidderminster, Worcestershire, son of a factory worker father and his mother was an auxiliary nurse. He had a sister who was four years older than him. He had a modest upbringing. His father was a reserved, self-absorbed man who had little room for sentiments of any kind. He, however, always took the responsibility to provide for the family with religious zeal and would mostly forgo his interests and needs for the sake of his family. Russell's mother was a loving woman who doted on his son.

When Damien announced his intention to join the army, his father was quite pleased and was proud of his son. His mother, however, had a distinct unease and occasionally tried to dissuade him from his plans but never forcefully. She was born during world war years, and her own father lost his life in the battle of Arnhem. She was two years old when her father died, and her mother never married again for the sake of children.

Damien's upbringing was nothing out of the ordinary. They never had luxuries, but there was always food on the table and life's basic necessities still catered for.

His sister, Jane, like her mother, was a caring and sensible girl. She was fairly studious and loved reading. She worked hard to become a teacher and followed her dreams with single-minded determination and eventually achieving them to the satisfaction of both parents.

Damien left school and attended a local college to learn basic engineering skills for two years. He joined an engineering firm as an apprentice involved in construction, fabrication and welding. During his apprenticeship, Damien thought about joining the army without declaring his intentions to his parents until he was finally accepted. He had a couple of really good friends from school, one of them Mark his best mate also joined the army with him. He served in Northern Ireland for a year and had several overseas tours of duty including Germany, Kosovo and West Africa. He spent time with several regiments and was finally commissioned in Royal Scots Dragon Guards at twenty-six. He rose through the ranks swiftly to become lieutenant. The 90's were drawing to a close, and the nervous excitement of new millennium was around the corner. He excelled in his role as a cavalry officer in Royal Scots Dragoon and was always praised for his dedication and looking out for his colleagues. He travelled quite a bit with army but would ever return to his hometown whenever his leave and duty commitments allowed.

He was tall with well-sculpted muscular but lean body; a fair reflection of his deep interest in exercises, keeping fit and healthy eating. The most notable feature was his clean-cut square jawline and intensely deep blue eyes; a trait he inherited from his mother's side. One of his friends remarked that he should try his luck in acting or at least modelling. It was quite flattering for him, but he would always brush this aside with a smile. Although he was a product of late 80's and 90's, but he would appear to carry the values of earlier decades, a much earlier period. He never smoked and did not overindulge in alcohol, traits he brought into the army life. He had modest success with girls mainly due to his shy nature which did not complement his robust physique and attractive facial features. His friends often raised eyebrows and expected more from him, but he was content with his lot.

By the time he was 21 he had one steady girlfriend, Laura, she worked as an occupational therapist in a local hospital.

His parents died within two years of each other after he joined the army, fairly early without any prolonged illness. Each time he was on tour of duty overseas and had to rush back to attend their funerals. His sister Jane had married a teacher, and they both immigrated to Australia shortly after her mother's death. Of the two parents, his mother's death affected him profoundly. As Jane left for Australia, no one was left of his immediate family in the country.

As the war loomed in Gulf for the second time in 2003, he was deployed with Royal Scots Dragoon Guard in Southern Iraq. His unit was involved in active combat and tank battles around Basra. Once the active battle was over, he was on a routine patrol with his two colleagues in a Jackal vehicle when he was severely injured in an incident in south Basra; his right leg had to be amputated below the knee. He travelled back to England for rehabilitation undergoing extensive rounds of physiotherapy, adjusting to life with a prosthetic limb and above all, finding his way in life again.

CHAPTER 11

Emma was hoping to take Damien somewhere where they could chat and get to know each other and learn of his war experiences. She was sure this had something to do with the deep sorrow in his eyes.

'*Fountainhead*' was a good starting point, but Damien himself indicated that he wishes to meet outside of this place. She thought about driving down to a small lake, she knew on the border of England and Wales. This will give them sufficient time to talk during the journey, and it will provide a refreshing atmosphere for Damien away from here. She asked Damien's acceptance first if he is willing to come along next Saturday.

Emma picked Damien from his flat; it was pretty nice and decent with several blocks of flats inside a perimeter with ample parking spaces and green areas. He lived on the second floor. Emma had not been inside his apartment. She called him before leaving home, and as soon she parked her car, she saw Damien coming towards her car.

"Hi, how are you? " Emma asked cheerfully.

"I am fine," Damien smiled, but she could feel that her smile could not hide his emotional strife.

"We are heading towards this lake and resort, about two hours' drive, should be able to get back by evening, is that okay with you?"

"Yeh" Damien nodded.

Emma was out of city limits and on to the motorway heading west in about twenty minutes, and she felt a bit more relaxed.

"So, tell me about yourself," it was an excellent time to start a conversation when they are not sat across, she thought.

"Not a lot to tell, I joined the army at twenty-four that was in 1996, along with my best friend, Mark. I have been to many places since getting a commission in the army, Northern Ireland, Kosovo, and West Africa, not always fighting off course.

I was in Royal Scots Dragoon Guards in 2002, and then moved to Kuwait then the invasion of Iraq in early 2003. We did not have many casualties, thankfully."

"How did you get injured," Emma asked with impatience.

"It was during a routine patrol in Basra; we were in our Jackal vehicle, three of us. We took a wrong turn and were ambushed. Our vehicle came under fire, grenade attack; it just exploded and was burned down.

One of my comrades died from his wounds. Mark was injured too and like me had to undergo surgery and then a long process of rehabilitation.

I survived the first attack, but I was shot in the leg that shattered my bone and part of the knee joint. There were complications during the healing process, and it got severely infected as well, the leg had to be amputated below the knee joint."

"What?" Emma turned in horror towards him.

"You lost a leg in the war, you never told me; It's so awful. I'm sorry that happened to you, it must have been horrendous."

"I had to get back home, had operations, then rehabilitation process, physiotherapies, had a prosthetic leg fitted. After a few tries, they got it right, and I am walking with this artificial leg now. I am quite pleased with the results."

Damien casually pulled his trouser a little to reveal his metallic prosthetic leg and Emma glanced at this in horror, keeping her focus on the road ahead was proving difficult, but she composed herself.

"Soldiers do get injured in the war, in peacetime as well. The pain was bad and never left me. I was taking a lot of pain killers for a long time, I managed to reduce this now." Damien said in pensive tone.

"Do you still suffer from a lot of pains?" "Yes, It varies"

"How did your family take all this."

"My parents are deceased, as this happened. Sister has immigrated to Australia; naturally, she was distraught, still writes to me and speaks to me on the phone. She asked me to come to Australia to begin a new life."

"I had a girlfriend, but unfortunately this did not work out, me being away for so long and then got injured and discharged from Army."

Emma could see the process of sacrifice, first putting his life on the line, then losing a leg, battling with pains and re-adjustment to life and then losing the love of his life.

"I still tend to get flashbacks of that day, wake up with nightmares, sweating."

"It was a terrible experience."

"Also, I was involved in an incident when I shot a young boy who was a non-combatant. This plays on my mind a lot; it was my mistake; I feel a lot of guilt about this."

Emma noted for this revelation, Damien hesitated quite a bit, trying to find the right words. She changed the subject to his likes, hobbies and the lighter side of his army life.

They got to the lake about noon, and there was a usual rush of tourists and day-trippers. Damien had never been here. Sun has come up, and there were only scattered clouds in the sky.

Emma began to note a mild limp in his right leg. He had gone through a lot, got a new leg and adjusting to life without one of his limbs, she thought.

"What about you, Emma." They finally sat down on a bench with a cup of coffee.

"I work in the city, investment bank to be precise." Emma took a deep breath.

"I am a financial analyst, numbers figures, money, currency, stock and shares, equities, unit trusts, ever changing trends in stock markets, world events affecting markets, that sort of things."

"I had a good friend, Russell; we were living together until five weeks ago in Brentfield."

"We had differences, he loved me, but some of his traits I could not cope with. He wanted me to slow down, start a family now; it was not working for both of us." Emma took a deep breath and continued.

"We decided to separate for a while."

"For a while!" Damien raised his eyebrows.

"Yes, for six months to be precise, see how we feel about each other and our relationship, the idea was mine. Russell wanted to wait and give me more time, but I could not live with constant expectations. I think this was the main reason.

We made a pact to allow ourselves time and space to see where we go. There is no compulsion on both of us; if life takes us in separate directions, there will be no blame on any of us, so we are quite free in our choices. We decided to meet and see each other after six months, and that is a firm promise by both of us, nothing else is guaranteed."

"So, you have another five months before you see him," Damien said in a reflective mood, but he admired Emma's honesty and forthrightness. "That's very good of you to tell me all about you and Russell and I wish you all the luck in the world, you are such a nice person."

They continued their chat after the meal. Emma noted that he begins to feel comfortable in her company and was talking freely compared to her meeting with him in 'Fountainhead'.

"How did you start in painting?" Emma asked.

"I was undergoing rehabilitation when it was suggested to me, 'art therapy' and quite liked it."

"Yes, I am also starting after a long gap. I used to paint as a little girl. My mum is quite good at this; she was an art teacher."

"Damien, did you have any psychotherapy for your symptoms? I mean you had a major trauma and now gets flashbacks; these are symptoms of post-traumatic stress." Emma said.

"I did initially; part of the rehabilitation process, the flashbacks and this burden of guilt has increased over time."

"Do you want me to explore this further for you, there are lots of new treatments and therapies available these days, I have read about these in the press and on the Internet."

"Yes, but I don't want to trouble you, Emma. You have your life, responsibilities, and you are busy. I am ever so grateful for your kindness and concerns; I have dealt this with this in the past and will probably ease off with time."

"I hope it does, it will be no trouble to me, perhaps a few phone calls, please let me do this." Emma pleaded with him.

Damien only nodded his head, and Emma knew this is sufficient, she did not want to corner him and changed the subject once again.

They spotted a lovely pub at the far end of the lake, and they wanted to have a drink. Their chat wandered through almost all nook and crannies of their life and Emma noted a smile on his face at last.

"You know, you look best when you are smiling." Emma was cheerful.

Damien smiled and nodded. They finished their drinks and headed home.

Emma felt so much better after this outing with Damien, at least he allowed her to read him, know his background, his feelings. She dropped him off at his apartment, came out of the car with the engine running and kissed him.

Emma, after this day, was drawn towards Damien and would wait for her art session to able to meet him. Damien appeared more cheerful than usual, and others begin to notice their friendship blossoming.

Damien would occasionally burst in laughter, change in his demeanour surprised him as well. He would wait for Emma to come on Thursdays and Saturdays. Emma had several chats with him; she finally convinced Damien to undergo psychotherapy once again.

CHAPTER 12

There were many common threads of interests between Russel and Pam and with each encounter, they would pick up these strands sub-consciously and be drawn closer to each other. Russell shared with Pam a love of outdoors, countryside, visiting historic sites, old churches, cathedrals, walks along rivers canals and above all flowers. He was learning more and more about flowers from Pam every day. She found his passion for boating, canoeing, kayaking, his knowledge of lakes and rivers fascinating.

Russell was a rugby player in his school days and still played the game. He loved watching rugby, tennis, cricket and football. His father was a keen sailor and secretary of local boating club. He probably instilled in him a love of boating sailing, kayaking and canoeing from an early age. Russell had a well-built trusted and narrow canoe which he named 'Tempest', and this would go with him wherever he went secured to a roof rack on his car. He would always find a spot where he could take his canoe. This gave him the freedom, a chance to go outdoors and as a means of exercise as well.

"Have you ever been to Norfolk Broads?" he asked Pam.

"No, not really dear."

"I was busy bringing up a child on my own, never got much chance to venture that far on my own, now this floral business," Pam said with a tone reflective of regret for lost time, and Russell could see her point.

"You should see it once, lovely place."

"I would love to" Pam smiled.

"Would you like to go there with me?"

"How about the coming weekend, I'll pick you up. We will hire a boat and go round 'Broads'." Russell smiled.

"I wasn't expecting as early as that, but I would come with you." Pam said with her characteristic beaming smile.

Russell greatly admired her genuine enthusiasm and her trust in him.

"I could go to the ends of the earth with you; you are such a lovely companion," She once said to him.

"This will be a rewarding and enjoyable trip; I can assure you this much." Russell was full of anticipation.

～つ

Russell woke up early on Saturday, it was a fine July morning, and there was a buzz in the air. Birds were chirping from dawn and Russell could tell from the noise birds make what sort of day it is going to be.

"They have an uncanny ability to sense what the weather is going to be like. For example, have you ever seen birds chirping when there is going to be rain all day." He told Pam one day, and she had no answer to that, and perhaps there was some truth in it?

"I would look out for this now and pay attention to birds call in the morning. "Pam had said.

Birds had started chirping at dawn and Russell could feel the smell of a beautiful summer's day in the air.

He checked the weather, and it was forecast to be a dry, sunny day, temperature expected to reach 26 c by afternoon, clear blue skies and no rain.

The days like these are few and far between and as a keen outdoor person, he knew this all too well to be ready with plans.

"Good timings" he mused.

He pulled in front of Pam's bungalow in his silver Audi. She was ready for him. He found her in her usual cheerful mood. She was gathering things in a picnic bag, drinks, snacks, napkins etc.

He was quite spellbound with her; she looked incredibly attractive and beautiful, wearing a green skirt, a beige blouse and a matching scarf. Russell could not take his eyes off her; He followed her to the kitchen where she was packing last bits in her bag. He put his arms around her.

She turned around to face him. He hugged her tightly feeling her bosom pressing against his chest, and she let him, He could feel her fragrance almost drowning him to a pleasant exalted state he never felt before. Pam patted and rubbed his back lovingly. She felt his firm sculpted body in her arms. She gave him a short peck on his cheek.

"Shall we move?" "Yes, off course."

Russell picked up the bags and put in his boot. Last-minute check on his atlas and then put the address in his sat nav and reversed out of her driveway.

He followed the A57 for twelve miles and then turned on A1 south taking the A47 turn off at Newark towards Kings Lynn and would follow the A47 all the way to Wroxham.

The day was bright and sunny as the birds have 'foretold'. Russell felt in great mood wearing a casual off-white cotton shirt with his favourite blue jeans. He had his sunglasses on to cut out the glare of the sun.

"Do you like photography, taking pictures?"

I like photography but haven't been taking many pictures lately, but I have brought my camera today." Pam said innocently.

"Oh, great."

"I used to take pictures until Peter was at school, sometimes I take pictures of my bouquets, floral arrangements, to keep a record for myself or send to a client but not that frequently."

"I hear that cameras are now digital; you don't need a film in the camera anymore."

"Of course, the roll film cameras will become extinct."

Russell continued on A47 past Kings Lynn towards Wroxham."

"Which one do you have? "Russell asked.

"I have a Canon Power Shot, it's a point and shoot compact camera, got a film roll from the high street, yesterday." She said casually.

"I can't believe this, you are joking."

"What." Pam was amused and surprised and that inquisitive smile spread over her face.

"What, what is so surprising?"

"That someone is using a compact camera in 2005 and still able to buy film rolls for this."

"Is it so surprising?"

"Yes, it is," Russell chuckled with affection.

"I have not used a film camera for the past six years; they are becoming a thing of the past."

"I just went to camera shop on high street and bought a roll of Fujifilm and have already loaded in my camera," Pam said casually, innocently.

"You are amazing, Pam" His tone was that of affection for her charming simplicity and naivety which so complemented her persona. She bent down and searched in her bag and then carefully got her compact camera out, holding it admiringly. Russell glanced at it and smiled.

"We will have great fun, 'Broads' are so photogenic.

I am using a Casio Exilim, digital camera, will show you." Russell said casually.

Russell thought, this innocence, just being her, plain and simple with a smile is so precious, so pristine and so powerfully beautiful, he will not have it any other way.

He was trying to figure out, while effortlessly following the bends of the road, how to phrase his thoughts and express them, in the end he gave up with a meaningful smile.

Perhaps whatever words he can conjure up would never be able to sum up, what he felt about Pam.

Just before Wroxham, he pulled in a car park. He opened the boot, got his rucksack out and pulled his Casio camera bag. Pam also got out of the car. Soft sunlight was filtering through the trees, and it was behind him. Pam wore a plain deep green skirt and a beige knitted top, hugging her fuller but shapely frame so nicely that Russell could not take his eyes off her and Pam felt this.

"What?"

"What are you looking at?" Pam felt his searching and affectionate gaze on her but he just smiled.

"Looking at you, looking so pretty and elegant."

"No one said this to me before."

"You need eyes to appreciate beauty."

"Can you stand just there, this morning soft light is always perfect for figurative shots with landscape, trees and foliage." He pointed to the spot and Pam took position there somewhat shyly as she had not been in this position for a very long time. She stood with a slight side on stance with one foot subtly behind the other.

Russell closed framed her against the woods and clicked just one shot and was looking at his camera screen and then waived to Pam.

"There you go, your first digital picture."

"Oh my God," Pam gasped in amazement. "That's incredible."

It was indeed a beautifully framed picture in a parking area with perfect soft light and capturing the early morning freshness and her radiant, beaming face with excellent clarity and saturated colours.

"No one could believe this was taken in a parking area along a busy road; you do have an eye for great photographs."

"Oh, thanks Pam, that's wonders of digital photography for you, I can now send this to you in email, make as many copies as we like, print them for you, without going to a camera shop.

You can also send it yourself or to anyone in the world with a computer, enlarge it, reduce in size if you want."

"I would love to have a copy, look forward to this." Pam said with a beaming smile.

CHAPTER 13

They reached Wroxham at about 10.30 am. This delightful place is usually full of tourists and day-trippers in summer and today was no exception. Russell knew the area well. Wroxham along with the nearby village of Hoverton is pretty much the centre of Norfolk Broads. This is where most of the boat hiring yards are located. Boats of all description are moored on either side of Wroxham bridge and can be hired for a day, a week or even for a few hours.

'Norfolk Broads' is a unique interconnected system of rivers, canals and waterways and some big lake like reservoirs. They were former 'peat holes' in ancient times and were later flooded to form these systems of 'broad lakes' which are in turn connected to rivers and canals. The soft flowing and relatively shallow rivers and waterways are ideal for boating and hence the abundance of boats on the 'Broads'. Russell had been giving Pam a snap introduction of the 'Broads' as he picked detailed maps of the waterways from the tourist information centre. He tried to explain the size and breadth of the place on the map to Pam. They walked over the Wroxham Bridge as Russell enlightened her about the geography and history of the area. He showed her several popular vantage points on either side of the bridge.

"This is a lovely place" they strolled down the place taking in views and taking snaps with their cameras, Pam with her compact 'canon powershot' and Russell with his digital camera, he felt Pam is slowly converting to be a firm admirer of this form of photography, but he admired her compact camera too.

He often stopped to show the images to Pam on his camera, and she would peer into his camera screen shading with her hands.

Her shoulder and occasionally, her breast would touch Russell's arm in the process, and he could feel a fragrance emanating from her and taking hold of him. There was such a surge of excitement and happiness inside Russell taking hold of his entire existence, engulfing him in a cloud of euphoria.

He managed to take several shots with her cannon compact camera while Pam tried her photography skills on his digital camera. She felt quite amazed and excited to see the pictures just taken to see there and then, secured in memory without the need for waiting a week to see the results.

He told her about the various boats available for hire here and where you could take them. People can hire a small dingy to medium sized boats to fairly larger vessels that can accommodate up to eight people on board for a floating holiday on the Broads. He hired a small boat with leather seats for four hours, "to be safe" he said. He helped Pam get in the boat first and then climbed over.

There was a small cabin with leather seats and further seats at the front of the boat to sit in the open. Russell showed her the controls and levers and reminded her that there are no brakes, to slow down and to stop you need to pull the lever back and to steer forward push the lever forward.

"It is as simple as that; I have done this before."

He checked the lever, controls and ignition and switched on the engine. The boat roared to life, and Pam immediately grabbed hold of the seat, steadied herself and sat down, smiling.

"There are no brakes, you pull the lever forward and back to control speed, the limit on broad is ten mph and some places even lower", he announced above the roar of engines, Pam nodded and smiled feeling she is in safe hands on the water.

The boat came out of the narrow dyke and then picked up some speed, staying on the right side of the river.

"I will teach you how to steer," Russell shouted, excitedly.

"Probably not, I don't think I can do this," Pam said with some apprehension.

"You drive a car, don't you?"

"But this is a boat; I never imagined I would be steering a boat."

"You will, a lot of things are done for the first time in life," Russell said in a cheeky tone.

Pam smiled; she felt more relaxed now as the boat glided majestically on the River Bure towards Colitshall. There were delightful bungalows with their lawns coming down to the water's edge, anglers sitting on chairs here and there with their fishing rods and lines.

Sun has come up now, and it was a perfect day, for sailing, photographing and just be outdoors. Russell steadily built up speed as they left behind the more crowded section of the river and headed towards Colitshall. Pam noted there were speed limit signs just like roads and navigable course of waterways were marked in some places.

Pam was relaxed and began to take in the views and enjoy this river 'cruise' with Russell.

"Broads are generally very safe, but you have to respect 'water' whether it is sea, beaches, rivers or here in the Broads." Russell said with some authority, and Pam nodded. She had her sunglasses on now and was taking snaps on both sides of the river, including Russell in the frame at times.

"The navigable section of the River Bure starts at Collitshall; we will stop there. It is a lovely village with a beautiful small thatched-roofed church."

Pam noted riverside pubs where boats were moored and people stopping over and getting into their boats.

The distance from Wroxham to Collitshall is about four and a half miles one way, and they were three miles down the river now. The water was crystal clear, they saw several mute swans gliding on the surface, and occasionally a grebe is seen diving in water for fish. The banks on either side of the river were sloping but not too steep with reeds growing profusely in some places. There was lush growth of foliage, dense trees followed by farmlands. Pam noted there are no hills to be seen here with fairly flat countryside on both sides. Pam admired his knowledge of the Broads, not to mention his boating skills and she felt in safe hands.

CHAPTER 14

Sun was up, and the sky was a deep blue colour with a few fluffy white clouds. A windmill appeared in the distance.

"That's a classic shot coming up for you, take one with my camera too"

He requested Pam. She was sitting on a red leather seat, but for this, she got up steadied herself and took a perfect shot of the front end of their boat, the river, beige coloured reeds and the windmill in the backdrop of clear blue skies and white clouds, a perfect picture.

"This is so magical, thanks for bringing me here." Pam said.

Russell switched on his camera and handed it over to her. "Look for the green matrix on screen, and when it appears steady press the button," it was a success. She was happy with her effort as she showed it to him, steadying her feet on the moving boat.

Russell slowed the boat down towards the right bank of the river. The green fields were gently sloping to the edge of the river. As the boat came to a halt, Russell threw the rope over and then got out of the boat first and tied the rope to a post. He managed to get Pam's bag and then gestured Pam to climb out and helped her out of the boat. He took her hand and she was in his arms for a brief moment as she landed on her feet and steadied herself.

The place was so idyllic, the day was perfect, and her companion was deeply and madly in love with her. Just her nearness, her presence and fragrance emanating from her body was enough to mesmerise him, and he could not take his eyes off her, and she felt this, felt his loving gaze on her. For so long she had been alone, abandoned so long ago by the man she married, she had forgotten how to be in love and now this, a deluge of attention and love, so quick and so fast. Genuine sincere and heartfelt affection and she did not know how to handle this, how to respond. Perhaps her beaming smile and her body language gave away so much, and this was enough for Russell and for her at this moment in time, at least.

She pulled a large grey towel and spread this on the grass and out came the goodies from her picnic bag, drinks, snacks, glasses, straws, napkins. Russell looked at her in admiration, how neat and well organised she was, so subtle and effortless, just so fluent in whatever she does.

"It's so peaceful here, enchanting I should say" Pam looked around.

Occasionally a boat would pass along the water with holidaymakers, young and old cheerfully waving at them and they waved back to them.

CHAPTER 15

Russell was lying on the towel, and his shoes were extending on to the green grass. Pam was sat very near him. He could smell the unique fragrance of hers, which only she can have and no one else could. Russell always had this thought as her scent immersed his senses so often.

He once thought of asking her what perfume or fragrance she uses but did not. He did not want this to be a topic of discussion, this has an ethereal appeal to his senses, and he did not wish to associate this with a brand of fragrance or that. What if this fragrance is her own or perhaps, he perceives it this way? Some things in life are best left where they are, unanswered, enigmatic, charming and mysterious, Russell thought and felt better about this. This drizzle of euphoria began to overwhelm him again. He put his hand on her shoulder, then her back gently. He could feel the outline of the tense strap of her bra at her shoulders and her back. This deluge of elation and delight was all over him, and he thought he was drowning in it: a pure heavenly, ethereal joyousness which nothing else could bring.

Pam turned to look into her intense eyes; she could read his innermost thoughts.

"Why do you love me so much, what's so special about me?"

"I am a divorced woman; no one ever looked at me like this or given me the attention you give me. Sometimes I feel, do I deserve it?"

"Yes, you do, Pam" You are so unique and very, very special.""

"I don't think there would be another person like you, not here not anywhere else on this earth or even in stars. I am certain of this."

"I am just lucky to be here with you at this moment in time after just a chance meeting. If I had passed this place to go further north for another interview and if I had got that job, I would not have met you. Or perhaps you have met someone and married him; I would not have known you, what a loss this would be to this earth, this human existence, my existence, our existence, this was perhaps meant to be this way. Your presence on this earth is a blessing, and I am just lucky to have met you, chance, and luck? Destiny? I think we were destined to meet; this was written in stars."

He sat up and looked into her eyes and then tenderly pulled her in his arms, very gently, feeling the soft suppleness of her body in his embrace and she let him. Her fragrance was his now, there was just a hazy blur of awareness. He could think of nothing else as her whole existence melted in his arms sitting on the grassy river bank. He kissed her face, then her lips. This happened so swiftly she hardly had time to respond, and she did not know what to do and how to respond. She seemed to lose contact with reality; her soul was drenched with purest rays of serene affection she never knew existed in this universe let alone will flood her soul like this. Few seconds felt like an eternity, time seemed to stop there.

"I could never let this go, this is the moment I was born for, and this is why I am on this earth to love this one person. I can live with her forever, a divorced mother of a grown-up son, a florist who runs *'Florarama'*. What people will say, the age gap, the social acceptance, I will deal with this. I would not care. She will be all I have, and that will be all I would ever yearn for, I would not wish for anyone else."

This downpour of joy completely and utterly drenched his soul and hers. He was so madly in love with Pam, a woman older than him, a mother who runs a florist shop at the edge of town. She belonged to a rare genus of people who only see the goodness around them, it just bounces off them like a swirl of fragrance and captivate all and everyone around them. Russell began to appreciate this simple, uncomplicated approach to life through the eyes of Pam. There were no doubts anymore. Pam has not gone out of her way to find someone. She waited and waited until Russell knocked on her door and now having found her, he would not let go of these precious feeling, these precious moments life had bestowed on him.

There were no doubts anymore.

She was there; in front of him. An epitome of contentment, beauty and endearment.

Someone who was raised in a strict convent, lost her parents early in life, whose husband left her for another woman with a child to bring up on her own. There she is, the most affectionate loving woman in the whole world without a trace of bitterness.

"You are such a lovely and sweet person, and I feel this from the bottom of my heart and soul. It is simply beyond me to contemplate anyone else but you."

"You love me because you are so nice and pure in your heart, I know this darling; I knew this on the very first day, I saw this in your eyes."

Time stood still, this whole place, the meandering shallow river, the thickly wooded forest, the sun rays filtering through to forest floor, the scent of wildflowers, the warmth of July sunshine and all sorts of buzzing summer noises around them were just made for them. To stand on this bend of the river, on this bend of their life's tortuous road, to feel this, absorb this and forever remember this. Russell was dazed with this ethereal delight once again; she ruffled his hairs as he lay in her lap, looking to the dark blue sky above.

"Shall we go for a walk in the wood?"

"I think we should. Russell jumped to his feet. He left the towel on the grass and picked up his rucksack.

There was an immense freshness in the wood. The sun was up now, sunlight filtering through to forest floor with all sorts of plants bushes and ferns growing here. They followed a walking trail through the woods and met several people along the way.

Russell got his digital camera out, his trusted Casio digital camera which he preferred on such excursions to a bulky SLR. He explained the working of a digital camera to Pam. "It only takes an SD card here in this slot; you do not need to worry about 360 clicks after this."

"Really"? Pam was amazed.

"You only keep the ones you like and delete the rest; it is as simple as that. He took a shot of purple wildflowers and showed the result to her. The image was crystal clear.

You can also edit the image, improve its colours, contrast and brightness as you require and save an edited image along with the original image at the same time.

Maybe I will get you a digital camera one day; it will help you to keep a visual record of all your bouquets and floral displays."

Russell said with so much affection in his tone, Pam could not say no. It was on her face, in her eyes and Russell knew this, no words were needed.

They returned from the walk after forty-five minutes, picked their stuff. Russell untied the rope, he helped Pam get in the boat first then climbed over.

Russell gestured to Pam to come and stand at the helm.

"You will be fine," I am standing behind you as he placed his hands on hers to steady her grip of the steering wheel.

The boat lurched and wobbled and then steadied as they begin to steer it down the river to a final couple of miles to Colitshall.

CHAPTER 16

Emma spent considerable time convincing Damien to undergo psychotherapy.

"It has been proved beneficial; these therapies have proved their worth not only here but worldwide, please give it a try Damien" she almost pleaded with him.

Emma had spoken at great lengths to him, what it entails, how long it takes, various types of psychotherapy, eye movement desensitisation and repositioning (EMDR) exposure therapy and even regression hypnosis. She also discussed issues of consent and was allowed to stay in specific sessions of psychotherapy if she wanted and Damien has no objection.

Dr Carter was an upright man of slim build. He had worked in several psychiatric hospitals and had thirty years of experience and specialised in trauma and post-traumatic stress disorder (PTSD).

"Post-traumatic stress was not so well understood back then," He told Emma.

He was a young doctor when PTSD cases first presented and began to be debated in medical circles and literature. Although recognised in World War I and World War II not much was known about this, symptoms were dismissed and sometimes referred to as shell shock on the battlefield. Veterans of war were expected to deal with it themselves and many did just that. It was after the Vietnam War when returning soldiers were studied and a pattern began to emerge. This showed the effects of extreme traumatic events in war zones and the battlefields of Vietnam. When the returning soldiers showed a high level of stress, social detachment and failure to adjust to life and society in general. Since then, accumulated experience over time and seeing war veterans over the years has paved the way for new modes of therapy to deal with this diagnosis. It is not confined to war only, any traumatic event in life including road traffic accidents can leave unpleasant memories which stays in a person's sub-conscious mind for a long time and continue to cast a shadow on the present.

Emma picked up Damien for his appointment and drove him to Dr Carter's clinic. This was an imposing Victorian mansion in leafy suburb of the city. The building was surrounded by mature tall trees. "The place looked so calm," she remarked, getting out of the car.

"Yeh," Damien was lost in his own thoughts. "You will be fine, Dr Carter is a kind and helpful person," she tried to calm his nerves. They checked in at the reception and were advised to wait.

Damien was all too familiar with this type of wait; doctors, surgeons, nurses, physiotherapists, pain specialist, he had been through it all.

The place where fairly distressed people come to seek, treatment, help and support ought to be welcoming and calming at the same time and in this room, she felt just that. She looked around and nodded in approval.

"Looks like a nice place." "Yes," Damien said softly.

They had to wait fifteen minutes before Dr Carter came out. He was immaculately dressed in a deep blue suit and white shirt with a bow tie. He shook hands with Emma and Damien. Emma noted his warm and firm handshake. "Please come in," he said as he led them through a corridor to a consulting room.

The room was well lit, had a large wooden table with a glass lamp, a desktop computer and several other equipment was laid out along with some files and papers. There was an impressive wooden unit behind the table packed with well-bound books and a few decorations items here and there. There was a triangular wooden mahogany wooden name bar facing the patient at this end of the table, it read.

Dr Jerald Carter
Consultant Psychiatrist
and Psychotherapist

He asked them to take a seat across the table. Emma noted he was trying to ease the tension as best as he could. He would be doing this day in day out with his patients, she thought.

"I read through your history about difficulties you are having since returning from the war zone. I have received detailed information in referral from your doctor and some information provided by your friend Emma, with your consent, of course," he added gently.

"I understand you are troubled by flashbacks of trauma, unpleasant memories of bad events you witnessed and endured during the war." Damien nodded in affirmation.

"First of all, I would like you to tell me this in your words as it happened. I know it will not be easy, but perhaps talking about this will lead to an understanding of your symptoms better. The aim of our various psychotherapies is to bring to the surface those sub- conscious thoughts, memories and even conflicting emotions and bring them to a more conscious level.

In a way, experiencing and confronting them again. You may have to undergo several sessions to achieve our treatment goals. We may use several forms of therapies, including EMDR and hypnosis regression. The aim is to achieve a state of mental relaxation to reach the layers of sub- conscience where these memories are stored and bring them to the surface, you understand that."

"Do you have any questions?" Dr Carter asked.

Emma and Damien looked at each other.

"No," Damien replied in a low voice.

"You may ask the question at any level of these therapies," Dr Carter reassured him. You may start now, he gestured to Damien.

Damien took a deep breath, looked around the room and then with his gaze downcast, began in a slow voice.

"I was in Royal Scots Dragons Guard regiment of the British Army. I joined in 1994 and had served in Kosovo before. We were stationed in Kuwait before the invasion of Iraq. It was

March perhaps when the battle started, and we were aiming to take Basra. It was after the main battle, probably in the second week of April 2003 when we were on regular patrol.

I think we lost our way and walked into an ambush; it was south of Basra. Difficult to remember what really happened, but we were stuck and came under heavy fire and grenade attack. Our vehicle exploded and burned down; both my colleagues were wounded in this attack. My leg was severely wounded from a gunshot wound to the right leg.

I was evacuated and received treatment, I don't know perhaps the heat of the desert, dust, don't know my wound did not heal well; the infection set in and the leg had to be amputated. There were chronic pains from right hip down to my stump ever since.

I spent three months in rehabilitation in the south of England, undergoing physiotherapy, exercises, psychological training for readjustment after this accident. I had a new prosthetic leg fitted. They did an excellent job, and they spent time with me so that I could walk again. I suffer from pain all the time but I have learnt to live with this."

Damien finished and looked in the distance, not meeting anyone's gaze.

"Did you kill any civilian?" Dr Carter asked abruptly.

Emma sensed the importance of this rather abrupt question and fixed her gaze on Damien to see his expressions.

"I don't know, I don't remember" It was all so quick, I was shot, my friends were shot and both of them were injured, one of them died later, don't remember much." He kept his gaze downward, occasionally looking sideways.

Dr Carter summarised and politely brought this consult to an end. He discussed and agreed the schedule of psychotherapy with Emma who was noting down all the dates and times and she was in a way responsible for bringing Damien to these sessions.

CHAPTER 17

Emma was patiently following Damien's psychotherapy sessions and noted some changes in his mood and behaviour. He was much calmer and not waking up in the middle of the night startled and distressed as much. He would still continue to toss and turn but managed some decent unbroken sleep. His mood was alternating between bright and sparkly to a flat affect where he would withdraw within himself and this concerned Emma greatly.

He had undergone several sessions of psychotherapy; both analytical and psychodynamic therapy and few sessions of EMDR.

Dr Carter had a detailed discussion with Emma and Damien about regression under hypnosis, a type of therapy where the patient is asked to go in deeper layers of consciousness under hypnosis and confront their trauma or the distressing events and try to come to term with this. Dr Carter was not sure of its success as it depends on many variable factors.

"It is worth a try", he looked optimistic.

Dr Carter had invited Emma with Damien's consent to be present in the room when he undergoes regression hypnosis, and she agreed.

"Will this be too distressing for him?" Emma sensed the importance of her presence to support Damien.

"It can be"

"I will try to explain. The storage of memories varies from person to person. We tend to live in the present, but our minds tend to wander in the past and sometimes in future. The human brain continues to filter out events and memories, some are consigned to the sub-conscience and not easy to recall. Hypnosis enables the mind to travel more easily across dimension of time. Regression is a process where therapist help induce a deep trance- like state and takes you to an earlier life, to the particular event or events that need to be explored. The human mind had somehow suppressed these memories in subconscious mind. These memories deep inside subconscious mind continue to cast a shadow on your present. It is these events in the past we need to explore, try to understand and address."

The room was dimly lit. Emma noted Damien to be apprehensive.

Dr Carter asked him to lie down on the couch.

"Damien, allow yourself to relax, with peacefulness, follow your breath.

Follow each breath to calmness. Let yourself go deeper.

serenity -- deeper -- deeper-- relax."

His voice ebbed down to more dreamy tones.

Emma could see Damien slipping into an altered state of mental relaxation or possibly sleep?

"You may feel sleepy, that's good, go deeper into this sleep."

"Deep breath, slow deeper."

Damien drifted into a trance, his arms limply by his side; head flopped over to one side.

"You can choose to go where you want to go, Damien."

"Damien" Dr Carter called out for him.

Damien remained in a sleepy trance; eyes closed.

"Damien, I want you to think about the day you got injured."

"Can you recall?"

Damien's lips mumbled, but no specific words came out.

"Can you see something, go deeper and deeper, tell me what you see."

Emma could see from the corner of the room; Damien was utterly static. His lips moved, some mumbling but she could not hear, he appeared to be in a complete trance.

Dr Carter waited for a few moments

"Where are you, Damien?" Emma could see Damien trying to say something, and then his voice became a little clearer.

"I am with Royal Scots Dragon. Our convoy is on a routine patrol mission in South Basra. Michael, my pal, is driving. I am in passenger seat, finger on the trigger."

"Where are you heading?"

"We seem to be lost, perhaps took a wrong turn. We are in a narrow lane. Dark and dusty street, all windows and doors are closed, no one out on the street."

"What can you see, hear?" "There is gunfire."

"Automatic sub-machine gunfire." "Where is it coming from?"

"I don't know, we are under attack."

"Big noise, then explosion, grenade attack! mine explosion?"

"I am thrown off the jeep, Mark is wounded, I can't get to him; he is on the other side of the street."

"There is gunfire from everywhere; our jeep is burning in the middle of the street. I run across the street and drag my colleague Mark to safety behind a wooden shack he is injured, the bone in his leg is exposed, blood everywhere, he is howling in pain."

"I locate the fire, coming down from the house opposite, run; we are getting after these fucking bastards."

Emma could see his head thrashing from side to side and his face perspiring profusely.

"We need to kill them finish them off, running,"

"blue door, kick the door open, gunfire and noise can't see a thing, kick the door open of first room, an old woman is yelling in her language."

"What are you doing, Damien?"

"Coming out, no one in the compound, someone moved behind the pile of woods in the courtyard.

I follow him."

"Is he armed, Damien? is he a combatant, a soldier?"

"I don't know."

"He is running towards the rear wall, trying to climb it,

I fire a burst of machine gun, he just falls like a dead weight, moves towards him, he is bleeding, face down, motionless."
"Is he in uniform?"

"No, I turn him over with my boot, blood gushing from his mouth, head flopped to one side, eyes rolling up he is lying motionless, only a kid perhaps fifteen or sixteen years of age. Oh my God, I have killed a child, oh God. The two women came out, wailing and cursing us, their shrieks are so piercing. "Oh God the older woman is perhaps his mother, she lunges at me."

"Then what happens?" Dr Carter asked.

"I slapped her across the face, oh God, she fell to the ground, smoke noise and blood."

"I need to run away from here, my leg is bleeding, the whole trouser is soaked.

"We are running in the streets, dragging our wounded limbs, doors closed, but the fire still raging, our vehicle in the middle still burning, running, running, oh God." Damien was thrashing his head from side to side.

"Damien!" shouted Dr Carter

Damien sat up with a jerk, his eyes closed he put both his hands on his face, his face was red and sweating profusely.

"You are alright, back home now."

Dr Carter gestured to Emma to come near him.

Emma put her hands on his shoulders, gently comforting him.

He was taking deep breaths, visibly shaken.

"Damien, it is me, Emma, you are here now."

Damien opened his eyes and then burst into tears falling into her arms.

Emma sat with him holding his head on her chest. It was shocking, just the thought of it, so frightening. How would it feel to be there, to see your comrades wounded and see yourself shooting an innocent boy in front of his mother?

It took an hour for Damien to come round from this ordeal, as Emma sat next to him holding his hand, comforting him.

Emma drove him home, tucked him to bed. He slept all the way through to next day, waking up momentarily then going back to a deep sleep. Emma was grateful that Dr Carter allowed her to sit through this hypnotic regression. She could see and feel glimpses of his trauma which Damien lives through each day perhaps.

"I begin to see this better now Damien" she mumbled to herself."

Damien saw Dr Carter for further sessions following on from his regression hypnotherapy, but after some weeks, Emma began to lose hope in this treatment.

CHAPTER 18

Russell accelerated his Audi A4 and joined the A1 from a slip road. It was a beautiful and crisp August day; the temperature was expected to reach 24 Celsius by midday.

Russell lowered the windows a little." I like some fresh air coming in when driving but feel free to control as you wish."

"I like it too", Pam nodded.

"Do you like me to share the driving"

"That would be lovely, see how we go."

Russell said with a smile.

He could feel the fragrance emanating from her again, so captivating, I could never get enough of this, he thought.

"The long road north" he muttered to himself. Whenever he took a road heading north, he had this exhilarating feeling come over him, sense of adventure, sense of discovery ?? perhaps both. Not that he did not like all the other roads travelling or going to different destinations directions, but there was something special in heading north as if going away from it all.

He wasn't sure but perhaps something related to pleasant motoring holidays in childhood with his parents when they would go up north from Lancashire to Cumbria then Borders, glens of Scotland and beyond.

"Do you have the same feeling, Pam?"

"You see meaning and beauty in all those small things, life is much richer that way," Pam said.

Russell turned on A66 at Scotch Corner.

A66 is an exceptional road, all the way to Penrith in Cumbria, the old roman road with some of the most beautiful countryside along the way.

"Ah! I love this road, green rolling countryside and moorland as far as the eye could see." Russell sighed. He was also aware of its dangers with sudden changes in weather as road ascends and dips and its unique weather systems accounting for many accidents, there was a warning sign right at the start.

"I remember travelling on this road when I was little, happy times!" Pam recalled her childhood memories.

Russell had driven about half an hour out of Scotch Corner when he pulled the car in a secluded and secure car park.

"Want to show you something" He knew of a small path which leads to a superb vantage point with spectacular panoramic views of the rolling countryside for miles around.

The day was turning out to be warm and crisp, and there was freshness of sort in air, few wispy clouds here and there only. Russell opened the boot and took out his waterproof jacket, "you never know in this part of the world, anyway there are some heavy showers forecast."

"I have got a rain jacket in my bag, don't worry." Pam said

He got his Casio around his neck. Russell led her to a cobbled pathway at the far end, walked for 200 yards with bushes almost touching them as they moved down, there was a slight ascent after this, Pam stopped taking some deep breaths.

"Shall we stop for a few minutes" Pam asked.

"Yeah, sure" said Russell.

She leaned and rested on a boulder as Russell surveyed the scene around them.

"Now" beaming smile, Pam got herself up after ten minutes. They walked further 150 yards down the path and then finally a turn to the left and a superb view, almost 270 degrees. The buzz of cars on the road was left behind, just a golden silence, a blue sky with misty haze in the distance and rolling green velvety hills as far as the eyes could see.

"This is so heavenly!" Pam got her camera out from her bag. She snapped several pictures.

"I want to take a picture with both of us." Russell was unfolding his portable tripod from his bag, secured the camera tightly on top, composed the scene with Pam in the picture, allowing himself space on the left of her and set the timer.

He pressed the button and hurried to her side and put her arm around her.

"Smile!"

He shouted and grinned widely as the camera clicked a few seconds later. He ran back quickly to the camera, reviewed the shot.

"Wow!"

Pam leaned into his view screen, her arm brushing his muscular shoulder. This was a perfect shot nicely composed with both of them smiling and the depth of field covering the rolling hills for miles in the background with blue mist.

"Have I convinced you to go 'digital' now" he chuckled.

"Yes, very much so, it's so amazing and ready to see immediately."

I can now send this snap to you in email or print a copy for you in fact as many as you like. Russell grinned.

"I would love to have a print, will always cherish this moment."

He took a few more shots with Pam from different angles and some landscapes with various settings. He loved the freedom of digital photography to take as many photos as he like. He gave his camera to Pam to take as many shots as she likes. "I will keep the best results; the rest can be deleted." She clicked several and Russell showed her how to view the shots taken, she was surprised with the ease of this new piece of technology.

They sat on the boulders, taking in the views, just silence with rustling of wind only. Spellbound in the magic of this moment, no man-made structures as far as the eyes could see.

"So timeless, imagine this scene a hundred years ago." Russell remarked.

"Not much changed, a very special place thanks for bringing me here, I could never have thought of this."

Russell sat next to Pam, holding her hand resting on her knee. They sat for thirty minutes perhaps but this looked longer than that.

They were at ease, at peace and this felt good. The scene was changing fast, dark clouds gathering from the west.

"I have checked the forecast; heavy showers then clear skies in the afternoon, although there are often localised weather systems here which no one can predict." said Russell

They decided to track back; Russell thought it will take half an hour to the car. It started to rain, and they both got their raincoats out.

Russell noted how steady she was on uneven ground moving with a grace he never expected. It started to rain heavy now. They got to the car, and the sky was deep grey shade with storm clouds, and the wind has picked up speed. The rain was coming down in sheets now, a torrential downpour creating puddles everywhere. There was sound of distant thunder and some chill in the air.

"Shall we sit in the back seat as the rain clears." Russell opened the rear doors, and they both got in, raincoats were all drenched as they took them off.

The waterproof jackets have saved them from a complete soaking. The rain was splattering on the windows of the car as if trying to come inside, seeking permission. There was some chill in the air, and they felt it. Russell had both arms around her and his head resting on her soft bosom. He could hear her heart beating and 'that fragrance' of hers rising in clouds and falling in a drizzle of ethereal delight over him. The windows were all misted, cutting them form time and space, here on a secluded spot on moorland on a Saturday in August; on a road that connects North Yorkshire with Cumbrian fells, the old Roman way.

Inside the car, time stood still. Pam felt his warm sculpted body resting lovingly on her bosom, his arms wrapped around her in a loving embrace. He had given in to her and she into him, there was no strangeness between them. Just like this little place in the middle of nowhere she never thought she would ever visit, she never dreamt of this moment when a man would be in love with her so passionately, which would come like a deluge and drench every corner of her existence. There was nothing on the horizon; she had been a mother and wife and a good mother and wife at that. Circumstances have put her in this position, she was a divorced woman not waiting for anyone young or old, she was content, accepted what fate had brought her. Living in the 'sequestered vale of her life' content, not asking for much. Here she was with an adoring and loving young man with his warm body wrapped around her, feeling every movement every rhythm of her existence and she feeling all his ebb and flows. Surprisingly it felt good nourishing and nurturing to the recesses of her souls which she never knew existed, let alone wanting to be saturated, drenched satisfied liked parched soil waiting patiently for an occasional downpour in the wilderness.

Russell had his face buried in her soft bosom and his arms holding her in his loving embrace, and he could feel her heart beating, his cheeks on the soft flesh of her chest and her unique fragrance sweeping over him. He felt her warm, supple body and squeezed her ever more tightly and felt affection flowing out of every pore of her body. She gently kissed him on forehead and ruffled his hairs with her soft fingers. Russell kissed her on her cheeks then her lips, soft lingering kisses and then her breasts ever so gently, nuzzling his face in her loving embrace as he did so.

There was a rain dance outside in all its frenzy, hitting the earth, catching the hilltops, creating puddles, breaking into little streams, pouring into rivers, the eternal cycle of life.

Inside the car with misted windows, there was silence as no words were exchanged, no words were needed.

Russell withdrew from her, looked into her eyes, dreamy eyes, deep eyes kissed her again rested his head on her bosom, she combed his hairs with her soft fingers gently as he drifted into a peaceful slumber.

The rain has eased off, and the maddening noise of raindrops on the car was dying down. Russell moved away from her, opened the car door and sat on his driving seat. Pam now sat beside him

"Shall we go?"

"yep"

It was a heavy shower, hopefully, some clear weather ahead.

They reached Penrith in two hours and then Russell turned his car towards Grasmere. She once told him how people visiting the lakes have one of the lakes as their favourite and she always loved Grasmere, and that's where they were heading.

CHAPTER 19

Emma had been following Damien's progress like a hawk. After the shock of hypnotic regression, Damien had further sessions of EMDR which went quite well. Some weeks passed, Emma noted that any improvements seen earlier in his demeanour are now lost, and Damien was relapsing again.

Emma had booked an appointment with Dr Carter, especially to go over her own thoughts and plans. She had read extensively around the subject of PTSD, especially in returning combat soldiers. She had learned that PTSD was less well understood initially but began to be appreciated more after the Vietnam war as more and more war veterans were noted to have symptoms of post-trauma stress.

In subsequent wars, in the Middle East and Afghanistan, more cases came forward. The cumulative experience of psychologists, psychiatrists and behavioural therapist in the USA, UK and other countries increased in dealing with sufferers of PTSD. New modalities and approaches to treatment evolved over the last thirty years. Emma was also surprised to learn that PTSD can become a chronic psychiatric disorder and can persist for decades or for a lifetime.

The training of combat soldiers demands them to be mentally and physically tough and expect them to endure and absorb such pressures and stresses. It is only natural that they deal with the effects of trauma and unpleasant events experienced or witnessed in the war zones and battlefields to their subconscious mind, which come to haunt them later.

Those who adjust to life after their military career, find alternate occupations, have a social support network of family and friends around them deal with this better. Those who have severe disfiguring injuries, loss of limbs, chronic disabling pains and especially have a poor social support network tend to deal with this poorly. These veterans are more likely to be unemployed, have an alcohol problem, have issues of homelessness and poverty and more likely to end up in a negative spiral.

Emma felt strongly from her observations that Damien is fighting four different battles. Post-traumatic stress, chronic pains, lack of social adjustment and guilt, the combined effect of these factors eating him inside and eroding him day by day. The loss of his parents, losing his trusted girlfriend and his sister's immigration to Australia left him with no social support network to fall back on.

He was like a boat cut loose and adrift in the ocean at the mercy of waves. She was very hopeful at the start of his treatment when he showed some improvement but began to be despondent and losing hope now with his relapses. She was particularly troubled by his guilt, causing much of his post-traumatic stress. If he could only learn to deal with his guilt, he could get on with his life and start the process of rebuilding it.

So far, Emma had shown enormous courage and immense resolve in providing him with this support which he lacked in his life till now. She just wanted Damien to undergo shock exposure therapy on her suggestion to resolve his guilt, perhaps this is what he needed. Thoughts were exploding in Emma's head but she was also aware that a hurried approach might complicate things. She needs to weigh up all the pros and cons. They have to take this risk otherwise Damien will never be able to come out of this bog where his mind and sub-conscience are stuck. Emma had rehearsed these thoughts and arguments over and over in her mind that her head started to ache.

When she entered Dr Carter's clinic, her heart was beating faster. She tried to calm her down but her inner strife was evident to a seasoned psychiatrist like Dr Carter.

He began asking general questions about her and Damien to put her at ease.

"I have come to speak to you about something significant; she went straight to the point. Please give me a yes or no answer. I am ever so grateful for the care and attention you have given Damien. However, he is not getting any better the way I expected it."

"I was thinking" her throat was dry and words would not come out of her mouth.

Dr Carter was noting her inner struggle and turmoil. She took a few sips of water and felt better.

"I was thinking," She paused for a moment. "I have not included Damien in this plan yet. I thought If I could take Damien to the same place where it happened, where his life seems to have stuck. His sense of guilt is eating and eroding him from within.

I am prepared to go to any length to lift this burden of guilt off him so that he can breathe again. Maybe confronted with the reality of the place he could deal with these traumatic memories better and perhaps be able to resolve them. I believe, being in that battle zone may provide the stimulus to his subconscious mind to bring these thoughts to the surface. I have read and researched the subject extensively, and I can become his 'de facto' therapist, for this I have to take Damien back to Iraq."

Emma took another sip of water. "I understand the risks involved, but I feel they are worth taking, and I hope Damien will agree too."

Dr Carter was patiently listening to Emma.

"Is it possible to confront these harmful thoughts and memories in the very place they unfolded, I mean in the lanes of Basra itself? The place where his army vehicle came under attack and the home where he opened fire in the fog of war and killed a young lad by mistake?" Emma finally summoned the courage to say what brought her to see Dr Carter today.

"This shock exposure catharsis may help confront those memories better; maybe he can make sense of it all and may get some solace, some answers, perhaps forgiveness and redemption and maybe some closure."

Emma's thoughts were now in free flow, and Dr Carter did not interrupt.

"Iraq is in a relatively stable state at present. It may be possible that his inner demons are exorcised that way. I have read accounts of people getting back to the scenes of trauma in battlefields of Vietnam, Afghanistan and Iraq.

Damien subconsciously holds himself responsible for the death of an innocent young person in front of his mother and is serving a self-proposed sentence. This guilt and self-loathing are holding him back, if this is resolved and reconciled, he could begin to take an interest in life and be able to love himself again."

Emma's eyes were misty as Dr Carter leaned forward and held her hands trying to make eye contact. "You are a courageous woman and has shown immense resolve, and I understand your point of view."

"The guilt is eating him inside. His self-torment will finish him one day." Emma's eyes welled up again.

"That is the issue, he takes some steps forward and then pulled back by his inner demons, those memories trapped in his sub-conscience are hurting him, he will get better, and it may take a long time." Dr Carter appeared optimistic.

"Yes, this may be tried, but it is fraught with dangers. You will be going to a place which has seen a lot of violence and bad things; it is far from stable there. I am concerned about your safety and welfare." Dr Carter expressed his caution.

"I know I will be taking risks for myself and Damien, but I want to give it a go for our sake. Damien has gone through the worse and is now at rock bottom, he can only get better. I can't see him disintegrating before my eyes. He is already psychologically damaged, what worse could happen to him? You have done all you could, I couldn't possibly ask for more." Emma composed herself.

"I must say you have shown enormous courage and dignity, and I wish you well. I admire your devotion to your friend and hope this turns out well for both of you, but I will have my reservations." Dr Carter said in a low voice.

Emma felt satisfied; she was not expecting a full endorsement of her plans; at least he did not actively discourage her.

Dr Carter was right; Iraq remains a dangerous place. Several armed groups were fighting to get military and political advantage in the ever-changing landscape of this war-ravaged country. British forces were still stationed there and US forces in the north of the country. Reports of suicide attacks, IED explosions, acts of violence are commonplace and ethnic divisions are ever deeper than before.

Dr Carter listened to Emma patiently. "I so much admire your dedication to your friend and your care and attention for him. I wish everyone can have friends like you.

"It is possible, called shock exposure therapy where graded exposure to traumatic memories is executed in a controlled manner. Taking back Damien to the scene of the tragedy appears quite extreme, and results can be unpredictable. This is a risky strategy, and you may put yourself and Damien in harm's way, I mean risk of physical and psychological harm." Dr Carter said in a matter of fact style.

"We have been through a lot" Emma's voice cracked. "I have read anecdotal account of soldiers returning to the battlefields and site of their harrowing experiences to seek solace and redemption. I have read some reports of soldiers who served in the Vietnam war returning to that country and found this a cathartic experience. I know German soldiers and their families, second and third generations making a trip to the battlefields on the eastern front especially *Stalingrad;* where their forefathers perished and suffered in most atrocious circumstances."

"Damien is standing on the edge; I can't see him dying bit by bit. If this continues, I will be consumed in this fire too, so I also have a vested interest in this." Emma's eyes were welling up.

"I want to give this a go for Damien's sake and mine." Emma broke down in tears.

Dr Carter stood up, placed his hands on her shoulders, comforted her.

Emma took a few moments to compose herself. She still has to think about logistics, visas, risk assessment, foreign office advice, and speak to retired military personnel known through family contacts who served in Iraq for information. She still has to convince and motivate Damien above all and then make travel plans. As she bared her innermost thought to Dr Carter and her audacious plan, she felt somewhat lighter and perhaps ready to tackle the upcoming challenges to put this plan into practice.

She requested Dr Carter to support her, provide her with details of Damien's history, diagnosis, psychotherapies, medications, his ups and downs and progress so far. She will be going to a foreign land with Damien to take a chance with fate, and she wanted to be well prepared.

CHAPTER 20

Emma was mentally exhausted after her meeting with Dr Carter. She was at least satisfied that he acknowledged the value of exposure therapy. She was not seeking the complete endorsement of her plans; he did express caution but did not discourage her. Paradoxically Emma felt somehow Dr Carter was silently praising her plans.

She managed to get quite a few things clear. First, he agreed that there is value in using this strategy to confront inner demons tormenting Damien, using shock exposure therapy. Her own extensive 'research' revealed anecdotal evidence that war veterans have visited the scenes of trauma as a form of catharsis. The more she read about the subject, more stories emerged that veterans and their families make an unusual bond with the place where their loved ones died or suffered injuries. Some US soldiers have gone back to Vietnam to seek solace many years after the war. The dust of time also helps to heal their wounds, and when they see the place has recovered from ravages of war, the intensity of their flashbacks and trauma somehow subside. There were also reports of people seeking redemption through other means such as charity work, help building school and helping children in war-ravaged areas where they once fought for their own survival. Their presence on the same soil where they faced life and death struggle and once considered enemies are now just another human being. This was not limited to recent wars.

Stalingrad was the most ferocious battle in the history of mankind and the most crucial battle of WWII. An estimated 900,000 people perished in direct combat, aerial bombardment cold and starvation in this atrocious battle which changed the course of human history. Wehrmacht elite sixth army was trapped in a deadly cauldron by the Red Army at Stalingrad and was asked by Hitler to stay put as he put in place a plan to supply the sixth army from the air. This was a flawed strategy as sixth arm gradually lost its fighting ability due to inadequate supplies, lack of food as the iron siege of Red army could not be broken. Both sides fought an annihilation battle to finish in the ruins of Stalingrad which Red army won through sheer determination and better adaptation to the most appalling conditions and sub-zero temperatures. The battle ended when 92,000 German soldiers surrendered to the Red Army in February 1943. Of these soldiers who surrendered at Stalingrad only 6000 ever returned to Germany six or seven years after the end of the war. This catastrophe had brought together a sort of camaraderie in the survivors of Stalingrad and their families. A constant flow of visitors from Germany to the Soviet Union continued each year to remember their fallen soldiers, to lay flowers on their graves and tend to war cemeteries.

After the fall of Soviet Union, this number has increased steadily and now consist of very few original survivors of the battle and mostly consist of their son's daughters and second generation of soldiers who once died in cold vistas between Volga and Don all those years ago.

Since the advent of the internet and increased global communications groups have been set up who remember various battles and bring the families of survivors to share their experiences and their grief in a positive way. Emma was surprised to learn that bodies of soldiers are still being dug up each year in Stalingrad some sixty-two years after the battle. Whether they are excavating for a construction project, laying the foundations for a factory, school or hospital or just digging farmland or building a home, bodies continue to surface in and around Stalingrad even today. The first task of the authorities is to identify bodies whether they are German or Russian soldiers, tracking down gradually to their rank, regiment, and eventually their name and identity using all modern methods and scientific tests available. Their families are informed, and they are buried with full military honours according to their nationality and allegiance. German war cemeteries have swelled up considerably in the last thirty years around Stalingrad as remains of more and more soldiers are unearthed. A unique phenomenon was also noted and commented on by lots of people in these internet forums. That of a 'shared grief' irrespective of which side you or your family member were fighting for. The battle of Stalingrad now happened sixty-two years ago, families sometimes second and third generation of fallen soldiers and survivors now meet each other. They share their grief over their shared loss, without any judgment on who was the aggressor or the victim. In fact, all were victims in one way or the other.

She learned from this exercise and knowledge that there is value in going back to the scene of trauma and seek some solace, some answers and perhaps redemption. She knew comparison can't be made with World War II, which was fought so long ago. Iraq war was a recent event, and the area is still under active military and guerrilla activity and political strife. There is also a vast gap in cultural history, traditions and religion of the combatants.

She managed to get all the reports of Damien's diagnosis, treatment, his full medical history and psychotherapies received so far. She would be on foreign soil and did not want to leave anything to chance. She had asked for help and advice from one of her uncle's friend Major Andrew Colby, who had served in Iraq and is now retired.

He was a major also in Royal Scots Dragon guard like Damien. She arranged a meeting with Major Colby and asked all the details she would need to get to where she wants to go safely along with a former British soldier. She also checked if she needed permission from MoD. She sought foreign office advice on travel to Iraq and precautions she needed to take. The official line was to avoid such a journey, but Emma had come this far and she had no intention of turning back. The most important conversation she had with him was about logistics.

"You need to get a fixer; someone who would be your guide, interpreter, security guard and driver and will oversee all your contacts and logistics. I don't see you making any progress if you don't arrange this. It should be done here before leaving for Iraq." He was clear and forthright.

Emma nodded in approval.

"I know of a British security company operating in Southern Iraq, and they will be able to arrange a fixer for you. You may have to pay this security company and this will hopefully remove the hassle of transactions of money logistics and other problems." Emma was ever so grateful and thanked Major Colby.

She spent the next week tracking down the company here in the UK and arranged all details with them. She had done her homework thoroughly to make this mission a success. She arranged ample leave from her company without disclosing the details of her intended journey. She had to take her mother into confidence who was horrified to hear of her audacious trip. She spent a whole Saturday pacifying her mother and win her approval.

Emma, having equipped herself with all the knowledge, wanted to put the plan in front of Damien. She booked a table in a restaurant and after a leisurely meal asked Damien if he would be willing to go back to Iraq, more specifically Basra and the actual scene of the traumatic events that have bogged down his life. Damien was at first ambivalent about the idea, but he was deeply moved with Emma's commitment. Emma could see his misted eyes and could not look at his face.

"Why do you love me so much, do I deserve this?" it does not make sense. You have your whole life and career ahead of you, and here you are ready to put your safety and your very existence on the line for me, why?"

"I don't know, I think we have to do this for your sake and mine." Emma had no convincing reply but her devotion to the cause was quite apparent to Damien.

"Sometimes, I feel you are wasting your precious life on me; you deserve better than this. I wish I could have met you in different circumstances and would have something to offer you." Damien gently dabbed his eyes and composed himself.

Emma felt tears welling up in her eyes. "You have already given me so much. You don't weigh or count love and affection by measures of this world; this is something beyond all this. I am a changed person because of you. I can't face my own conscience if I don't go that far to get some solace and redemption for you, to seek some closure."

"I will never be able to repay your debt, Emma." Damien put his hand on Emma's, and she looked up as their gaze met.

"You don't have to, there is no debt, I am doing this for you and me also, it's my vested interest too." She looked long and hard into his deep blue eyes and knew he understood, no further explanation was needed.

CHAPTER 21

It took Emma two weeks to finalise her arrangements to fly to Iraq via Istanbul and Amman. She had made contract with the fixer in Basra, who will come to meet them at Bagdad airport and will then travel with them on internal connecting flight to Basra. Their visas, currency and debit cards to be used were all arranged through her agents. She was carrying enough money to sustain them through thick and thin for a couple of weeks.

She had paid for the services of fixer through the British security company, and there were to be no financial dealings with the fixer inside Iraq. She would only pay the British security firm directly and that too inside the UK. This was extremely important as she would be helpless if unreasonable demands for money arise there and she may not be able to meet them.

Their fixer's name was Husham Bin Marwan. She had spoken to him over the phone and insisted on getting all his details including his address, phone number, national ID number and his most recent photo. The security company as a go- between made sure that all these details were verified and passed to Emma, while copy of this was kept by the security company.

She spoke to Husham on the phone, she insisted on having some password between them to verify his identity when he meets them at the airport. He laughed at her extra cautious approach, but Emma was dealing with this in a matter of fact style and would not settle for anything less. She briefed Damien on some aspect of her plans.

Damien's experience as a soldier was no use to them now. He was part of an invading army and needed no permission, visas, currency safety and security guarantee. Here he was going as a civilian with a female friend, whom he only met three months ago; it was a big difference, a huge difference indeed.

Emma had done all she could to make all arrangements made in time and as smooth as they possibly could be. Although no one can give her fool proof security and any provision she had in place may prove to be bogus or invalid, it's a risk she was prepared to take otherwise this trip would perhaps never happen.

She had even made sure that all medicines given to Damien for pain relief are with them in adequate amount and had documentary proof of their legitimacy as they would pass through various countries to get to their destination.

Their flight was uneventful but tiring, a full 18 hours including connections delays and airport transfers. They were received by Husham Bin Marwan, their fixer, at the airport and Emma made sure he is the person she had to deal with. Husham was a well-built man of about forty-four and like most Iraqis sported a moustache. He greeted them with customary Arab warmth for their guests. They stayed in a hotel in Baghdad overlooking the Tigris River which flows through Baghdad. It was almost two years to the time when this city was bombed heavily in 'shock and awe campaign'. Extensive construction work was ongoing, but ravages of that bombing campaign were still visible. There was a haze in the air which Emma found out was due to sand particles suspended in the air. The glare of sunlight was too much to bear, and Emma had to wear her sunglasses almost regularly. She had a long chat with the retired Major Colby she met in England before coming here; about the sensibilities of local people their customs and traditions and gained some information herself.

Emma came prepared with loose baggy dresses, scarf so that she would not stand out from the crowd. She had bought few unisex *'shemagh'* from Amman airport, the chequered Arab scarf which she and Damien could both use. She had some unassuming black jeans and trousers and loose cotton shirts which came down to her knees.

Husham was an interesting man, very talkative, spoke excellent English in Arabic accent and was sometimes too loud for comfort. He had extensive knowledge of Iraq's history which he would gladly demonstrate on the slightest pretext. Emma noted that he does not mention the two gulf wars where this country was the epicentre and war was the reason she was here with Damien. The last war just happened to be less than three years ago. Emma and Damien had a good rapport with him. Landing in Iraq were two different experiences for Damien and Emma. He had been a fighting officer in a war, the legitimacy of which is still being questioned far and wide and he spent considerable time here before being evacuated after his injuries.

Emma, on the other, had never been to a Middle Eastern country before. She found the heat stifling and glare of sunshine was unbearable at times.

They rested and slept nonstop for 12 hours. Their connecting flight from Baghdad to Basra was in the evening, allowing them enough time in bed. They were picked up by Husham in the evening to get to the airport two hours before their flight. The flight duration was one hour but added security meant they have to be at the airport much earlier. Emma had changed her clothes and had her *shemagh* around her neck and loosely covering her upper body as well. She was wearing black trousers and a light- yellow cotton shirt coming down to her knees. Damien was in just jeans and a white shirt. Husham sat further back from them and Emma felt relieved as she did not wish to speak to him in the plane and draw attention.

Emma and Damien did not speak during the flight; they were lost in their own thoughts. The trip to Basra took precisely one hour, and they were met by a car and driver pre-arranged by Husham. Their hotel was a five-story building, reasonably modern and clean with air conditioning.

As they were being driven to their hotel in Basra, Emma noted some unease in Damien.

As the streets of Basra passed before his eyes, he began to have flashbacks of his time here. Emma wanted him to see all this with his own eyes, this was part of his exposure; this was part of the plan.

Emma wanted to have a meeting with Husham without Damien being present. She gave him the time of 6 pm in the lobby of the hotel. Emma was comfortable as it was sufficiently spacious to have a chat of this nature.

Husham was on time; he ordered tea for both of them. Emma began slowly and went over the whole episode of trauma and psychological harm he had suffered, his suppressed memories of that fateful day and his burden of guilt which is eating him inside. She was empathetic and mindful in her choice of words and her tone as not to offend Husham's sensibilities and feelings. After all, this country had endured an invasion by more than one nation this country had no quarrel with. In the process, they had thousands of civilian deaths and continue to pay the price of the war even today. She explained and put emphasis on redemption from his guilt.

"If we could only find the family, the home where he killed an innocent young boy by mistake in the fog of war; this exposure may help him to confront his inner torment", she explained to Husham in simplest words she could think of.

"If the mother or family of the boy could forgive Damien, he would have some solace in his life."

She described how Damien is continuously tormented with these thoughts and is so full of remorse and so far, no therapy has helped him.

"I understand and will try to help him." Husham was honest in his offer of help.

Emma gave Husham detailed information of the day, time of the day, address, name of the place description of the house. She gave him information on all surrounding landmarks which he could gather from Damien and one of his army colleagues she met especially for this purpose. She also described the house with a rustic blue door where Damien shot down an unarmed Iraqi boy.

Emma had some hope, but not a lot as the pace of events in this war-ravaged country is so fast. Deaths, a gun battle and explosions which took place nearly three years ago had little meaning in the psyche of people who are faced with these events on a daily basis. It was sad and depressing, and she felt she could do nothing about it.

She wanted to take Damien in the lanes where his 'Jackal' came under grenade attack and machine gunfire. She had obtained one photo of the burning vehicle taken perhaps when Damien and his pals were rescued and the name of the street from extensive research of her own as she asked so many of his colleagues for help. This has to be a gradual exposure, and Husham understood her request.

It took Husham two days to get back to her. He had identified the street and tracked down the family whose young son was shot down. Emma thanked him and prepared Damien to visit this place. She insisted on changing his outfit as well and asked Damien to wear a *shemagh,* he already had a stubble for several days, and Emma was quite satisfied with their outlook.

Husham was due to pick them up the next day, and they had to be ready by five in the evening. The sun cools down a bit at this time and was also the time when the incident took place on that fateful day.

CHAPTER 22

Husham bin Marwan was a perfect match for the role of a helper and guide. He was their driver, guide, interpreter and security guard. He had tracked down the house where Damien had gunned down a non- combatant Iraqi boy. He told Emma in a slow hushed voice that he had seen the family and the mother of the boy is willing to see Damien. He had shown the map and location of the house to Emma.

At 5 pm, the sun was low in the sky and evening began to cool down a bit but the air was still. Husham pulled in front of their hotel and drove them to a neighbourhood in south Basra. Emma had toned down her appearance; she was wearing a long white cotton collarless shirt coming down to her knees, loose black trousers and the black and white Arabic scarf 'shemagh' around her neck. Damien was casually dressed in beige pants and a white short-sleeved shirt.

Husham stopped the jeep some distance away from the street, they got off and followed Husham. Damien could feel some familiarity with the place. Dusty lanes, homes leaning on one another. Boisterous children were playing football in the streets, yelling loudly as they kicked the ball around, some were wearing Chelsea and Manchester United shirts. They moved through a narrow winding lane then turned a corner to a broader path, and this was the place. Damien stopped, this was the very place they were ambushed, memories came flooding in, flashbacks of a lengthening evening, they took a wrong turn and could not turn back in time, looking for an escape, gunfire from all sides, explosions, smell of sulphur in the air........

Emma sensed his inner strife but did not want to intervene, not now anyway. She knew from his reaction that they have reached the place which keeps haunting him. This exposure should happen; this is why they travelled all the way to be here.

"It was here our vehicle came under fire, it's here we lost one of our pals, terrible…." Damien mumbled.

Husham had also stopped some distance away from them, allowing Damien time and space to deal with his memories, his emotions, and Emma was grateful for this gesture.

Emma and Damien continued down the lane, few people were gazing at them from behind doors, through windows wondering why these people are here, what is so special about this place. He stepped forward another thirty yards, the rustic blue door was still there, its paint further erased and peeled, few remnants streaks of colour remained but still well recognisable. Damien stood in silence for few moments and looked around.

"It was here; Damien pointed to the door a bit covertly and said in a low voice. Husham waved and came closer, "yes this is the place you were looking for, I wanted you to find out yourself." Surprisingly he was himself speaking in hushed tones.

Husham asked Damien if he is in the right frame of mind and still wishes to see the mother of the boy.

He allowed time again for Damien and Emma and stepped away from them. Emma and Damien stood not facing each other's gaze, contemplating and then conferred for few moments in a slow voice.

Emma finally nodded to Husham; he came and put his hand on Damien's shoulder to give him support and courage. He stepped forward and knocked on the door, the same door which Damien and his pal broke down with their boots in the heat of the battle.

A younger woman answered the door, and Husham explained the purpose of his visit, he was now talking in Arabic though in much slower voice. He waited for a while and the same woman appeared in the door again, this time opening the door wide open. Husham stepped inside the compound and gestured Emma and Damien to come in. They silently moved inside, and the young woman closed the door behind them.

Sun was just above the horizon; shadows were lengthening now, but there was still light in the sky. This was a sombre moment and carried an enormous burden. Damien had come a long way to face this moment; he could not back out now. He slowly moved forward with Emma, head still bowed, avoiding the gaze of the whole place perhaps.

The memories flooded back and he could remember the place well, sounds of gunfire, looking for combatants, eyes scanning every corner, someone hiding behind a pile of broken furniture and wood, some movement, women yelling frenetically and someone running towards the south perimeter wall. A volley of gunfire, sound of a thud as the man falls from the wall and lying in a pool of blood. Damien steps forward and push the dying man with his boot, finger tense on the trigger. He was barely sixteen years old, blood flowing out of his mouth, chest and head; more yelling from the boy's family. His comrade pulling at his arm to leave, he withdraws fast and is back in the alley, his vehicle is on fire, he fires in all direction, and they run toward the far end …

Husham said something loud in Arabic and Damien came back from his flashback. An old-looking woman in baggy almost ragged dark clothes comes out in the compound, young woman beside her. There were few chairs, a tripod stool and a bench, Husham asked her to sit down and gestures Emma and Damien to sit down.

Damien was still avoiding the gaze of old Iraqi mother. Husham took control of the tense situation, shifting his eyes rapidly from Damien to the old mother. He explained to her in Arabic why this former soldier is here, "he is seeking forgiveness". The last sentence delivered in animated gestures with both hands scurrying and he repeated this again, bending down to search for the gaze of old mother to make sure she understood and then added." This foreign soldier is so full of remorse and seeks your forgiveness."

She began with a low voice and then as if reliving the moments, looking at an empty place not addressing anyone in particular, her voice became louder and clearer.

"There were explosions, smoke, firing everywhere, not from my home, we are simple poor people, my son was not a soldier, he was fighting no one."

Husham translated this in his accented English for Emma and Damien.

"Then foreign soldiers broke the front door, I was yelling and crying, telling them to go away, they were everywhere, there was so much noise, smoke. "My son was hiding there", tears were running down her weather-beaten wrinkly face, she used her scarf to wipe some of the tears, He was hiding behind the pile of wood, waiting for the soldiers to go away."

"Then what happened." Husham encouraged the old woman. "He ran towards the back wall to escape," she gestured to the back wall as if this happened yesterday. "I don't remember, there was so much noise, gunfire. He was lying in a pool of blood; I ran towards him his eyes were going up closing down, he was mumbling and then he was gone. I shook him to wake up, speak to me, his head was in my lap blood gushing from his head, chest, I just cried and yelled, his head just flopped over, don't remember much."

She wiped her tears again. There was a stunned silence in the compound as if a tragedy has just happened, and they can see it by turning their heads.

Husham took charge again, "Bad things happen in war, people die sometimes innocent people. This solider says sorry for what happened to you and your son and ask for your forgiveness. The soldier did not know he was so young and innocent." Old woman said something mumbling, Husham was taking his time as Damien did not hear any translations, he could see clearly with his own eyes as if able to understand every word she is saying.

Husham said to old woman, "God will give you *peace*, he was a good lad, God bless him."

"He wanted to become a mechanic, he liked cars and trucks," there was an anguished gleam in those dark eyes for a moment then her head bowed again. The anguished mother continued to reminisce in her son's memory.

These words felt like a lightning bolt to Emma, here in this compound thousands of miles away in a foreign land in an alien language in fading light she could see a mother's dreams shattered forever. What is the difference, pain of such a devastating loss is pretty much same everywhere, she thought for a moment, and her own eyes welled up.

The grieving mother lifted her head and wiped her tears again with her scarf.

"This soldier, here was shot in the leg and one of his young comrades died in this lane, their vehicle had a grenade attack." Husham like a skilled negotiator was presenting the loss of the 'other side'. They are here to grieve too, your son Yusuf, pay him respect and ask for your forgiveness." The old mother had now composed herself. Emma felt she was not very old, but grief and circumstances have worn her down. Husham suddenly pointed to Damien's leg and asked him to show his leg, Damien hesitated for a moment, but Husham came rushing towards him and lifted and rolled his trousers to reveal his prosthetic leg and bending down and gesturing towards the old woman said "His leg was wounded by fire and then cut off." Old woman looked at this strange-looking biomechanical leg. Damien saw the awkwardness of this comparison; the woman lost her son, and he lost his lower leg as he gradually rolled his trouser down with his head bowed...

The woman looked towards Damien and Emma said, "I forgive everyone, just hope my son is in paradise."

"God willing, God willing" Husham repeated his blessings in Arabic.

Husham and old mother talked for a while in Arabic, without Husham turning towards them with any translations. He finally turned around and said to Damien and Emma.

"The mother wants you to come with her to her son's grave" then adding, "it's not far from here."

Damien and Emma looked at each other, no words, just silence, nodding. Husham led them down a narrow lane and turned left at the end, and they were outside the built- up area after ten minutes. The sun was setting fast, and there was an orange glow in the sky. There were some cultivated fields, sheds of farms animals and their feeds stacked up, date palms were swinging in a cluster against the orange grey sky. The old woman was coming behind them, supported by the younger woman.

Husham pointed to the graveyard behind the date palms. A small three feet perimeter made with blocks and mortar made out the edge of the cemetery. There were several graves here, small and large some made out with mounds of sand and earth few were cemented with flowers scattered on them, only fewer had a headstone with a name. They waited at the edge of graveyard for her to arrive and waited till she entered the courtyard first.

She reached for her son's grave as Emma and Damien followed on Husham's gesture. Emma had put *shemagh* to cover her head now. The old woman offered prayers at her son's grave, and they all raised their clasped hands in prayer, in the fading light, the glint in her eyes was easy to see. In the reflected orange glow of the sun on the horizon with lengthening shadows, this solemn ceremony carried enormous significance.

A mother's prayer for her son and a foreign soldier seeking forgiveness and redemption, Husham said a few verses in Arabic without translating them at the end. The mother rubbed her hands on her face to end her prayers and looked content.

They trundled back through dusty streets to the woman's home. The woman continued to say something which Husham said were prayers for their safe return home. The light was fading fast now, and it was getting dark. Husham asked Damien to wait at the door as the woman wanted to give him something.

"What could it possibly be?" both Emma and Damien thought. She came out of the darkroom behind the compound and had a faded silver medallion in her hand, it was worn out and not a round shape with a rustic chain. It has some eroded marking of letters, "This will give your heart some solace and peace."

Husham nodded to Damien to take it. He bent down, embraced the old woman and thanked her for her forgiveness, her magnanimity. She put the ancient medallion in his neck and touched his forehead. Damien could see dried down tears on her wrinkled face as he saw her deep eyes from close, the eyes that would have shed many thousand tears before.

Emma was gazing at the old mother as she touched Damien's forehead and saw some peace descended on her weather-beaten face. Damien needed this moment of redemption and forgiveness to finally get a release from the shackles of self-torment he chose for himself as perpetual punishment. At this moment suddenly something dawned on Damien and perhaps Emma at the same time. This Iraqi mother who lost a young son in the war is also suffering from PTSD, unresolved grief, never given a diagnosis, no EMDR, no psychological counselling and there was no mention in the local press. At the most people asked her to accept her fate and consider this *Allah's* will and show '*sabr*' and she as doing just that or perhaps she was waiting for this moment for a final catharsis, to seek closure. Emma and Damien in a paradoxical way brought this catharsis, this closure for her. The glint in her eyes when offering her prayers on the grave, dried up tears on her cheeks, weak smile of gratitude and small medallion she gave Damien were her final rites, and she could now lay her son's memory to rest.

Husham said goodbye to the old mother and thanked her personally on behalf of visitors as they slowly moved towards their vehicle. Damien turned to look back once at the rustic blue door; she was still standing in the doorway.

CHAPTER 23

Russell visited Pam several times, sometimes on Wednesdays helping her in *'Florarama'* in the afternoons. He would become her assistant for the afternoon, opening boxes, laying out flowers, ornamental grasses, leaves, arranging vases and helping her with creating beautiful floral displays under her watchful guidance. She was so proud of Russell's contributions and always admired his quick learning and artistic inclinations.

He would ring the metallic bells in the front room with her permission knowing there are no customers on Wednesday afternoon. She would smile at him with the sort of amusing charm mothers reserve for their children doing something brash but allowable.

Sometimes over weekends, they would go out for drives, eating out in old pubs and trendy restaurants, going for walks visiting historic buildings, cathedrals, country fairs, floral exhibitions, walks along canals and rivers, art and craft shows and movies too.

"I could go with you to all these places, you are such an ideal and knowledgeable companion." Pam complimented him quite often.

Russell had asked her interests and her wish list of things she always wanted to do. Russell was aware, she was a working mother, keeping her life together was her first priority. Now she was settled in life but now hardly had time or space to go and do things on her own. She told Russell about her interests in watching live performances of classical music, operas, stage plays and musicals but has never been away to such events in over thirty years, almost all her adult life.

"Would you go to see a stage play or musical with me?" Russell asked directly.

"Yes, I would, I think I can," Pam said with her characteristic beaming smile.

"Okay, deal! we would go to see a musical or a stage play; I will look out for this and will make a dash for it."

Russell spent some evenings and afternoons with her at her bungalow. He had invited her over to his apartment but only after putting some extra effort at cleaning. He would make sure that he had some decent cutlery and crockery and cooked some really nice foods to appeal to her taste. She was always magnanimous in allowing his bachelor's existence to be an excuse for his haphazard way of living. He was drawn ever so close to her, truly a soulmate, the thoughts of Pam occupied him a lot.

She once said, "If you are on a long train journey and you meet a stranger, start a conversation of mutual interest and a 'bond' develops between two people. This leaves a positive mark on your soul, your mind. You may not meet this person again; the imprint of this brief encounter will still enrich your existence."

"Life is a collection of days, months, years and above all moments, we can't own time, it always moves forward. The trick is to filter out bad experiences and hold onto good ones and in a way magnify them, everyone should try this." Pam had said to him.

The more Russell thought of her, the more she was endeared to him, and she became part of his existence ever so silently. Slowly and subconsciously he was drawn ever so close to her, and always had this overwhelming desire to be near her, talk to her for ages, hold her, kiss her and feel her fragrance around him overwhelming all his senses.

She could read his mind, his emotions, even what is going through his mind at any given moment, and this always surprised Russell.

"How do you know all this?" he would chuckle on those occasions.

"I know you!" was her usual and brief answer with all the emphasis on 'know' delivered with a beaming all- knowing smile which made it all too meaningful.

Russell noted he was waking up fresh, had a spring in his feet to get to his office in the morning. He was overly effusive and friendly to everyone, and this was noted meaningfully by his colleagues. There were speculations, but he had no news for them if he was seeing anyone or dating, someone. Russell wasn't remotely interested in many of his eligible female colleagues. He would still attend office parties, social events and would go out with some friends he had made. It was his secluded world, and he was pretty happy and content in it.

The thought of Emma crossed his mind often.

Where did he go wrong? What could have been done better, whether he will see her again? How will they feel about each other? Has she met someone else? Did he unwittingly put pressure on her? Should he have waited longer to take things to their natural course? At the same time, part of him was content that he did bring the issue to the front, had a frank discussion about it rather than waiting for things to happen. His chain of thoughts would move to how she is now? Has she found anyone? Is she actively seeking a relationship or just waiting? Does she miss him? Or think about him?

How would she see his friendship with Pam?

Thoughts! and more thoughts! A whole procession of them until his eyes started to feel heavy and he drifted to sleep.

～つ

It was Friday evening; July was drawing to a close almost three months since he left Brentfield. This is summer at its peak in Britain with flowers in bloom, days lengthened to allow long day trips. He searched around on the internet to see if they could go for a musical or a stage play. There was nothing nearby. He searched for Shakespearian play being staged but nothing was being staged in nearby places. He saw Shakespeare's famous play 'Midsummer Night's Dream' but that was quite far away in Royal Shakespeare Theatre, in Stratford-on-Avon, 'about 137 miles, not that difficult' he thought.

There are plenty of daylight hours, they could easily reach there, see the performance and still turn back.

He phoned the theatre and booked two tickets. He did not check with Pam if she would go?

What if she declined? Then what, I will cancel the reservation and get some partial refund. She would love this, and we will have a great outing. He was prepared to take a chance.

He thought about the logistics, if the play ends at 10 pm it will be difficult to travel back home in time, possible but it will be a hard push, certainly would not like this after a pleasant evening.

So perhaps book a hotel room as well, sound right, but he was doing this all-in anticipation that Pam would agree and come along. After getting all the bookings, he called Pam.

"Would you like to come along and see a Shakespearian play with me, I have got two tickets?"

"Yes, I would love to, where do you want to go?"

"So be ready, I will try to pick you at 9 in the morning."

Russell was too casual and did not tell her where they would be going to. He hung up but felt a guilt creep over him. No, she trusts me wholeheartedly, and I must reveal the whole plan to Pam, there should be no ambiguity.

He phoned her again, "Hi Pam, we are going to Stratford, and this will take about three hours to get there. I think I mean it is quite possible that we may be a bit late getting back, so allow an overnight stay in a hotel !!! a possibility." He completed the sentence with some hesitation, finally.

"Okay", reply came in her shrill voice, and Russell felt over the moon.

～

He reached her home at the usual time. She was dressed in a grey-black patterned skirt and a white blouse; the morning showers have cleared, and the sun was out again. They got to Stratford in less than three hours and it was a pleasant drive.

"Have you been to Stratford before?"

"You would love it, your kind of place." he said with some assurance. Russell had been there once before with friends when living in Brentfield. He, somehow, had an exciting feeling that this place perfectly matches her in every sense, elegant charming and still down to earth and Pam would love it here.

"No dear, I have not been, would love to see it all with my dearest and ideal companion. She complimented Russell. You know I love to travel with you and now begin to see the world in a different light, you make me so comfortable, and at ease, I could travel with you to the ends of the earth and not get tired ever."

Pam said in a dreamy tone of affection and adulation with her loving gaze on him. Russell felt an immense joy of overwhelming proportions surge inside him.

"Thanks ever so much, I wish I could choose the right words to convey my thoughts." Russell chuckled with delight.

"I know you." Pam smiled with her usual exuberance.

Stratford, situated on the banks of River Avon, Shakespeare's birthplace is a picture-perfect town of immense charm, no wonder tourists flock to this place in droves. As this was a weekend in August, it was packed with visitors from all over the world. Russell and Pam visited Shakespeare's birthplace, an incredibly well-preserved timber-framed building housing a small museum and then Anne Heathway's cottage a short distance away where Anne, Shakespeare's wife, lived as a child.

They had lunch at a restaurant and then settled on a bench on the grassy bank of river Avon seeing the world go by. That was much-needed rest for both of them.

Pam was smitten by the charm of the place. "I have heard about it but never been here, you are such an excellent companion. I don't think I would have come along this way, nor there is a friend who would come here with me" Pam was so innocent in her assessment.

They had a lovely leisurely stroll along river Avon before the performance in Royal Shakespeare Theatre. Russell showed her the imposing building of the theatre from across the river.

The play, 'A Midsummer Night's Dream' was thoroughly enjoyable for both of them but more so for Russell. He sat with Pam and could feel her fragrance overpower him to the extent that he would lose focus on the play. His shoulder was rubbing with hers, and occasionally he would lean on her bosom feeling her softness pervade into him.

She felt this intense affection for him touching her soul so tenderly it stirred her to the core, and she felt weak inside, giving in to the most exquisite feelings she had for years perhaps for the first time in her life. She did not withdraw and let him touch her tenderly, allowing his arm and shoulder to rest on her bosom, whenever. He would hold her hand for hours, squeezing them lovingly, and she reciprocated his touch, his affections.

They were back at the hotel after dinner, and it was the first time, he was with Pam in a room other than her home. There was no strangeness, no awkwardness between them just respect love and fondness. It felt that way, they have known each other for centuries, their whole existence was meant for this nearness waiting for ages all those years for this summer's night in Stratford-upon-Avon. No words were exchanged, and none were needed, just a hazy blur of awareness as they came close to each other. That night they slept soundly, waking up and then drifting again to most peaceful sleep imaginable, clinging to each other holding softly, holding tightly, like a drowning man hold on to a passing raft. Like barefoot weary travellers crossing deserts and valleys of thorns for days on end find themselves in a lush, tranquil valley of incredible freshness and plenty.

They paused at every step, ran down each gully, each nook and cranny turned every corner and soaked this incredible love exuding from its every pore, coming down in streams from every hillside and becoming a deluge. This daze of euphoria lit up every corner of their existence, touched places they did not know exist within themselves until now.

This is what love should be,
this is what love ought to be,
complete and unconditional,
spontaneous and natural,
love not attached with strings and caveats,

not coming with ifs, buts or regrets,
not seeking labels of social acceptance.
love that is not yearning
to belong to a social matrix,
social matrix that is presentable and
acceptable to the world, society
deep, pure untainted love
deep spiritual love
which, only the union of souls could bring.

They found this love in the most unusual of circumstances in the arms of unlikeliest of companions they ever hoped to meet in a lifetime. They felt complete, enriched and fulfilled.

CHAPTER 24

Shades of Endearment

Since his return from Stratford, Russell was in an exalted state of mind. His body and soul were in a state of ecstasy he never felt before in his life, not even with Emma or before that. He felt floating in the clouds, an intense jubilation permeated his soul. This exhilaration overwhelmed him reaching far to the nether recesses of his soul, his existence; places he never thought existed in his mortal being, or they could be touched so tenderly. He was unaware of such elation before in his life or in other people's life.

His life has followed a typical convention so far. Family, school, friends, university aspirations, ambitions, girlfriends, first love, break ups, bust-ups, weekend parties, sports, jobs.

Then the first serious relationship with Emma, jobs, his hobbies and his desire to settle down. Nothing prepared him for this. Even in his wildest dreams, Russell never thought he would come to love a sweet, charming, soft-spoken simple and innocent woman so profoundly. Someone who has been married and divorced, and that she will quietly walk into his life and he will feel so helpless. All his thoughts will give in to her, long for her; seek her nearness, her fragrance, her soul, her companionship.

Was he dreaming? And will he wake up and come face to face with reality? He wished to remain in this 'world', in this drizzle of euphoria forever, it was simply beyond his control to think of anything, anyone else. He was not breaking any social mores or promises. She was not attached to anyone and loved her as much; otherwise, he would not have felt the way he was feeling. He was unable to think of life without her, is it possible? How would she respond? His thoughts ruminating through his mind again and again, and each time the verdict was the same.

It was September now; days were cool but pleasant with some warmth and occasional sunny days.

Russell was meaning to tell all of this, bare his soul to her. What is the best place, not at *'Florarama'*, not away from her home? She would like to be in her own environs to listen to this, feel this and be able to respond. He could not dream of causing her any discomfort, any harm, howsoever slight.

He asked Pam if he could come and see her at her home, she agreed and asked him to come over on Wednesday when she closes *'Florarama'* in the afternoon.

He drove to her place. Pam was waiting for him, dressed again in exquisite clothes as usual; a navy-blue spotted skirt and light grey-blue blouse. He found her in the living room. Russell settled on the sofa; soft afternoon light was filtering through in her neat living room. Birds chirping in her garden could be heard inside the house.

"Would you like some coffee?" Pam asked.

"I could never refuse your coffee; it is always so excellent." Russell followed her to the kitchen, he put his arms around her, "I so much love you! it is so difficult for me to put this in words. I am not very good at expressing myself."

"I know, darling, I know this; I knew this from the first day I met you. I see this in your eyes."

"Pam, I want to say something to you, do think about it, I am not seeking answers right now. I wish to be with you forever, I can't think of living a life without you, ever."

Pam turned and looked at him as if she knew he has come to say this today. She knew he would say this one day, perhaps very soon, and as he walked in, she could read his eyes betraying his emotions.

"I have loved you so dearly, so unconditionally, and so have you." She held his face in her palms. This is pure, true love, pure unadulterated love which does not care for consequences, it just happens."

She gave him the cup of coffee as they moved to the living room, she sat next to him.

"True love will probably never reconcile with our social moorings, it never does. This social matrix is so essential for our survival, our day to day existence. True love has no place in the social array we all pledge our allegiance to. This true and pure love strikes like a flash, in fleeting opportunities, in brief encounters and sometimes through back doors. From time to time, it shows its golden promise and those moments are precious."

"But we need our social moorings and our place in this social matrix to find our feet in this world and make sense of the chaos around us. Get an education, live a decent life, be recognised socially, get a living, hold a job, look after and support our children. Most people don't find this love ever and when they do find it, they are are unable to break free from their social moorings."

Russell looked into her deep eyes and said, "I have not felt this type of love before, I feel so helpless, we are not attached to any 'moorings' and are not bound by any promises or social restraints." Tears were now streaming down his face as he understood the meaning of her words.

She looked at his face for a long time and took her time.

"In a way we are," her eyes now welled up too.

"I do not wish to drag this beautiful relationship within the confines of an accepted social matrix, this would be hard. Putting a label on it and bring this to become part of the social matrix even harder. I may not remain the 'person' you have come to love so dearly.

These are 'shades of endearment'; we can't always attach a label to them. Each and every affectionate encounter in one's life plays a part just like a bouquet, every strand, every petal, every leave, even dead ones make up the bouquet, contribute to the overall effect.

I have loved you so dearly, no one can take this away from us. Most people don't get a chance to feel this type of pure selfless love in their entire lifetime. We are among those who have found it, lived it. I don't see much difference in loving someone from the bottom of your heart for two months, two years or twenty years for that matter; it always remains a part of you and enrich your life."

She placed her cup on the side table and moved closer to Russell, held his hand in both her hands and looked in his deep blue eyes.

"You know, when I was a little girl, I got hold of a butterfly. I was chasing it and then caught it. The butterfly was fluttering its wings in my grasp to break free. My dad saw this and asked me to let go of butterfly. He sat me down and said 'butterfly only looks good free and flying from flower to flower, you may get some satisfaction now, but butterfly will be damaged and you may not like this yourself."

"Some moments are like butterflies, they come along with their richness, their colour and beauty. They dazzle us. If we try to hold on to them, capture them, own them, they get tarnished, and you may not like what you have collected over a period of time."

"Do you feel men and women who seek extramarital affairs or similar fall in the same bracket?" Russell asked.

"No dear! " Pam took a deep breath.

"It all comes down to the purity of intent. Neither you nor I were seeking each other. It just happened; perhaps it was meant to be that way; there is always a reason for everything.

Love and lust have a very thin dividing line, and for the onlookers it is often blurred. In fact, an iron wall separates them.

There are 'affairs' which are 'divine' and there are marriages which are 'illicit sordid binding contracts', love never goes to waste, it always leaves a mark, a legacy, that's how I see it."

She had finished her coffee and noted Russell was not drinking from his cup anymore after taking a few sips.

She moved closer to him and hugged him to her chest, putting her hands on his back rubbing gently, comforting him.

"I have never been loved, cared for, so tenderly. You have touched me so deeply, it is so hard to put this into words, far better to just feel it. This will always enrich our lives no matter where we are, what we do. Nothing and no one can erase these memories, not even time." Pam's eyes welled up again, but she showed great restraint and forced herself to smile and chuckle.

She pulled him away by his shoulders and held his face in her soft hands, looking deep into his blue eyes.

"I think, I can let you go now, on your own journey, to belong, to find your feet in that social matrix. Everything happens for a reason; do you believe in this old phrase." Pam chuckled again.

"I have lived my life, but you have a lot to live for. You may wish to have children one day or perhaps soon, a home, your own social moorings, they make us complete."

"I don't want to have children," he said in a low voice.

"Why not," she was sparking now.

"I would love you to have kids, you will make a wonderful father. You still have to see Emma and see how things develop," she searched for his gaze and only stopped when he nodded a little.

"The time spent with you is the best part of my life, howsoever brief, and always will be. Again, it was meant to be that way, that's my belief. In a short while I have lived a lifetime and will always be grateful for this, will always be grateful for your love and companionship, you are my soulmate."

"I will always cherish these lovely embraces, your care and attention, your deep selfless love for me, no one can take this away from us. It will enrich our lives, and we will reminisce about the good times we had."

Pam's words tore through Russell's heart, tears were now streaming down his face, and he was inconsolable hiding his face in her bosom once again and making her blouse wet. He could see the wisdom in her words and so much admired her honesty, but the overpowering grief of losing her was too much for him.

She held him with his shoulders once again looking deep in his eyes and gave him a loving shake.

"Now, no more sadness let us enjoy the time we have. I will make another cup of coffee for you."

"That would be nice." Russell forced a smile.

∽

Russell met Pam a few times after this, and he began to respect her honesty and integrity even more. His intense love for Pam now had philosophical dimensions without constraints of time.

She was so right in her assertion that he can't own time and fix all the variables to his liking. He may make a decision today based purely on honourable intents and with a clean heart, but this may not survive the harsh questions life may pose in future. There is a real risk that he might damage the very soul, the very person he loves so tenderly and yearned for.

Pam's words, *"I may not remain the 'person' you have come to love so dearly, so tenderly"* reverberated in his mind and gave him solace and comfort.

Memories and experiences will always remain pure, untainted as they leave an indelible mark on our souls which no one can erase, they will make us a better person, and everything happens for a reason. His musings gave him conviction, hope and courage as he began to make sense of it all. His pact with Emma, his flight north to get away from his past and his chance meeting with Pam. She would often hold his face in her soft hands and extract promises that he will meet Emma with open arms and see what life brings. Russell would just nod.

"You will be very happy, I have this intuition, and I am certain of this, you will see."

Her beaming smile would make him feel better, and he would put his arms around her hugging her tenderly, feeling her beating heart and her heavenly fragrance. These were their moments, their very own 'shades of endearment'.

CHAPTER 25

It was the first week of October; next week it will be six months. Russell had asked for one month's leave from his company well in time and was granted; his intense hard work was greatly appreciated, and he was entitled to three weeks leave and requested an extra week as non-paid leave.

There was a chill in the air and leaves were turning yellow, ochre, beige and red in this part of the country. Soon all leaves will be gone, the eternal cycle of life, all elements they are made of will return to earth.

Russell thought about Emma, how will she be, how she looks like now? Will she still want him, has she found someone? Thoughts constantly doing a merry dance in his mind. How will she see his friendship with Pam.?

Saturday 15 October 2005, he called Emma, no response on the first ring, and then he dialled a second time.

"Hi! it was Emma at the other end with her characteristic shrill voice. "How are you Russell!"

"I am fine, how are you."

"Did you miss me? "Indeed, I have, I am dying to see you.",
her voice cracking.

"How was life for you?" Russell was apprehensive.

"Oh, I am a changed person Russell, I miss you terribly, I was
not kind to you. I am so sorry; I was not kind to you." Her
voice cracking with emotions.

"Don't say that Emma, it was a mutual decision, a pact."

"If I knew what I know now, I would never have let you go out
of my sight, and I let you go for six months," Emma started
sobbing on the phone.

"I know, I know you" Russell comforted her.

"I have got a month's leave starting next Friday and will talk
and exchange stories, I have a lot to tell you."

"I am driving south and will look to book a place to live for
four weeks near you."

"There is no need for this, Debbie is away to Australia for six
weeks, she has given the keys to me; you will stay with me
here."

"That's great; it's a big hassle to rent a place for a short time."

Russell and Emma chatted a dozen times that day, and old
magic was back in their lives, without even seeing each other.

Russell set off in his Audi A4 on 16 October down his familiar
A1 and got down to Emma's apartment in little under four
hours. He only had a couple of breaks for coffee. The moment
he pulled in her block of flats and opened the car door, Emma

came running towards him, tears running down her cheeks and she was hugging Russell frenetically, Russell had his arms around her.

"So then," she looked fresh and radiant,

"you look great" Russell complimented her.

"So do you, Russell; I am so happy to have you back, it was my naivety."

Russell and Emma chatted for the whole week, late night in bed, over breakfast, on long walks, on long drives, in restaurants, cafes and shopping centres.

"I have been to Iraq and back safely," Emma said suddenly.

"What the hell! you are joking, what were you doing there? this can't be true." Russell sat up flabbergasted.

"I was on a mission to save a life and perhaps save myself." The story of Damien stunned Russell. "If I had the vision which I have now, I would never let you go", Emma could not control her tears. "If I lose my job tomorrow, it will not matter, I see life from a different perspective now."

"You were in Iraq!! Russell shook his head in disbelief, why did you put yourself in harm's way? you did not inform me either."

Russell found this hard to believe what he was hearing.

Emma went through the whole saga of Damien's struggle with PTSD and the enormous burden of guilt he was carrying.

"It became my own struggle to pull him out of this dreadful quagmire, I almost forgot my own self, it became my mission, but I don't regret this one bit as it showed the sides of life, the resilience of human mind and soul and fragility of life. I value each moment of life now; I became less critical and more optimistic; I am a changed person Russell, believe me! because of this experience.

"It was not a life and death situation, I would have honoured our pact, but this journey of life in the last six months opened my eyes to see things beyond our immediate existence. First seeing Damien's struggle on several fronts just to stay alive and his disintegrating life right in front of my eyes then all the psychotherapies he had. Cognitive behaviour therapy (CBT), psychodynamic psychotherapy, EMDR hypnosis regression, he had them all. Then travel to Iraq; seeing the actual locations, battlefields and finally coming face to face with the mother of the boy, shot by Damien. This gave him that redemption that forgiveness, he was seeking. He had a big change in his demeanour, taking more interest in life, and looking forward to rebuilding his life. I just happened to be there at the right time of his life to give him that support; if not me, someone else could have done this."

"Damien believes I gave him hope to live, and this is a great satisfaction for me. I met him a few times at 'Fountainhead' and he looks more positive. I have urged him to see Dr Carter once at least to see how he should approach his treatment and whether he needs further sessions of psychotherapy, hope I will convince him. I have not met him for two weeks, I just wanted to give him time and space to adjust what transpired in Iraq and hope this will be for the better."

Russell reflected on the harrowing experiences Emma had, "you have shown enormous courage without any desire for personal gains, and I can see this.

In a way, I am now happy that I didn't know where you were, I would be worried like hell." Russell said with genuine affection for her.

"I think I need to go over this Iraq sojourn quite a few times to grasp it, just listening to you raise my hairs on end."

"Oh yes, I don't know myself how I did it.

This was an extraordinary situation." Russell just gasped at the thought of going back to the battle scene and confront the family of someone who was shot dead.

"I nearly lost hope at one point when all therapies, especially regression hypnosis, failed to address the issues he was facing. It was out of utter desperation I suggested this to Damien."

"The last throw of the dice." "Yes, pretty much so."

"You know what, Russell, I discovered myself a lot with this journey, there are lots of potentials talents, call what you like, lie dormant within everyone. Given some careful attention, some conviction and they spring to life; we should explore and see what we are capable of."

"Yeah, I was teaching Pam how to steer a boat on the river, she could not believe this was possible, but she did fine."

"Did you love Pam?" Emma looked up.

"I did, very deeply so, but I won't' be able to put this in words, in any bracket, it was a different kind of love, just a different shade of endearment, perhaps what you experienced with Damien, I don't know."

The difference is, it was me who was wandering in the wilderness, and she stopped for me, held me and guided me like a bright light in the dark. If I am sitting here with you today, it is because of her. She wished me and urged me to seek my own social mooring my own love in life and just carry all the positives from my encounter with her. There were times when I made up my mind to be with her, but she dissuaded me from doing that. I realised the value of her judgment, her wisdom and above all her selfless devotion, it is so difficult to describe I will always be indebted to her and perhaps I am a better person now than I was. All relationship leaves a mark just like every flower, every petal, every blade of salal grass, fern leaves they make the bouquet of life complete, love never goes to waste, that's how I see it now." Russell said with some introspection.

"Pretty much the same analogy Damien used once when I saw him apply layer after layer of paint on his canvas. He said, every brushstroke counts in the overall picture even if you paint over it."

"Yes, very much so, we were miles apart but perhaps having the same spiritual experience."

"Not only this Pam would only see the goodness around her, pretty uncomplicated approach to life, she was left by her husband to bring up a child, worked all her life, but there was no trace of bitterness."

"That's her steering a boat on Norfolk Broad". Russell showed Emma a snap of her which he took on River Burr near Colitshall.

"That's interesting, she looks elegant and graceful and bubbly too." Emma was so full of praise for her.

"When I was coming down to see you, Pam asked me to give her love to you and asked me to make a promise, to bring Emma to see her. You would love her I am certain of this and her *'Florarama'*, it's just magical."

"I would love to meet her."

"You Know Russell, these six months have turned my world, my philosophy of life upside down and this is for the better. All I wanted to do is climb to the top, best company best position best, fringe benefits, to the exclusion of all else, I would stop at nothing and will gamble all to get what I wanted. I gambled on losing you forever, how bad it can get. Now I don't care, if I don't get the position get the promotion, hell with it I am not in this race any more. Yes, I will do my best and will not flinch from dedication and hard work but in the right order of priority."

"I will have children, lots of them," Emma laughed.

"I may get out of shape that's okay will try to deal with this, what I don't want to do is live with the fear of failure anymore; it is okay to lose some time.

If I lose my job, my career is derailed, I will take it, deal with it, will bounce back from adversity. I don't mind if people say look, she has thrown away a glittering career for the sake of having babies, I will just smile that's what I have learned from life. Those who truly love me will see me through all this and those who don't perhaps I don't need them. People get this sort of wisdom in a lifetime often when it is too late to have an impact on their life.

I am so lucky to get you back Russell as it was me who pushed you aside to think it over. I won't let you go anywhere now."

"Not just you, Emma, we all look towards perfection or what the world around us see as perfection, just a little bit more, just a little bit more." Russell said with animated gesture. In search for that extra one penny, we forget the ninety-nine we have. I was looking to complete my life, our happiness with having children, a settled existence, a 'perfect life' as defined by the world around us. There is no perfect life.

Life's currency is time, and I begin to value moments now. If children come along, I would be over the moon, if they don't, I will not feel bad at all. The inner happiness, calmness and contentment bounce off you to the people around you, just reflect from the next person to you. It's okay if someone does not share your way of thinking, let them be, allow them time to find their own wisdom in their own time. That's how I feel."

Emma just looked at Russell, her eyes misty as she fell in his arms sobbing uncontrollably, sometimes wiping her tears and smiling. Russell hugged her tightly and kissed her.

CHAPTER 26

Emma pulled her Peugeot in front of Damien's tower block. She buzzed several times for his apartment on the call system but did not get any reply. Emma feared he may be taken ill or moved to a different address. She had no other means of contact; he did not carry a mobile phone.

After buzzing and waiting for ten minutes, she pressed the button of apartment number six directly opposite Damien's apartment.

Finally, someone replied.

"Hi, I am sorry to trouble you, Emma was apologetic, I am buzzing the call bell for number five apartment for my friend Damien, there is no reply; I am concerned about him."

A sleepy male voice appeared on the system, "Oh that gentleman in flat five, I think he probably left, I will come down."

After a brief period, a young person with stubble and wearing shorts came to the door. He appeared sympathetic.

"I am sure he is not in the flat, he was probably evicted." The man said avoiding eye contact with her.

Emma felt a jolt of intense sadness mixed with indignation. Someone who lost his leg and his hopes on a faraway land for his nation is now just a homeless figure where his neighbour was kind enough to come to the door but knew nothing more about his whereabouts.

"Do you know where he could have gone?" Emma asked, hoping against hope.

"I think he was made homeless," but could not elaborate why he was saying this. Their glances met, and Emma understood why he would come to such a conclusion. There was no further conversation between the two, and the man stood in silence; perhaps himself laden with guilt for deserting his 'obligation of care' to his neighbour.

"Many thanks, sorry to trouble you." "Ok, mam, I hope you find him."

The drizzle was turning in to heavy rain now, the chill of late October evening made Emma pull her coat tightly around her. She began to turn back from the door.

"You should also check under the bridge," the man said in a heavy, husky voice but avoiding Emma's questioning gaze, who turned back to face him.

"I mean some homeless folks live there, for a short while, you know."

"It is just down the road, about fifteen minutes' walk." he pointed with his hand.

Emma could not say a word; the man delivered the whereabouts of the friend she was trying to find desperately.

"Thanks, many thanks."

"Take care," the man shut the door behind her.

Russell was waiting in the car; the rain was now falling in sheets; car engine and wipers were on. Emma was getting wet walking a short distance to the vehicle.

"He is not there, probably evicted from his residence for non-payment of rent." She said in a matter of fact style or perhaps sub- consciously suppressing the gloom of the situation and putting a brave face.

Russell was taken aback.

"What do you mean, evicted? He must have an alternate accommodation." Russell muttered to himself as the reality began to dawn on him as well.

There are worlds within worlds, there are rules to follow, norms to conform, bills to pay; there is little room for personal sympathy even if you are a war veteran. People could die in their homes without their neighbours realising for days. Despite the best intentions, there are many holes in our system where vulnerable people can slip through the net. Provision of all social care through a regimented system of health and social care has its downsides; the community's collective responsibility is non-existent. Everyone assumes that such and such department and such professional will be doing this, it is their job.

That's why no one checks on their vulnerable neighbours for simple things such as checking they are safe, have enough milk for tomorrow, picking their medicines from chemist, all need to be done by 'state' and 'professionals'.

"Where could he possibly be?" Russell said to himself thinking about his possible whereabouts.

"I don't know, I will call the community psychiatric nurse tomorrow, or perhaps I get a call back to my message this evening."

"The man at the apartment said, he may be sleeping rough, and we could check 'under the bridge' where homeless people take shelter," the word barely coming out of her dry mouth.

"We can go and check there; we can't leave this for tomorrow."

"Do you think it is a good idea," Emma appeared a bit apprehensive.

"I mean there are drug addicts, people with infections and some mentally disturbed people in such places."

"We should at least try, we'll be fine." Russell pulled the car out in pouring rain.

The bridge the man mentioned, Emma had seen before. It crossed the main road diagonally and had large wide arches. Trains crossed the bridge in both directions, and there was electric meshwork on top and weathered black bricks gave it a forlorn look. Graffiti artists were at work here, and rubbish was strewn everywhere, giving the place a desolate look.

The walls were painted with lettering, images slogans and messages, some in bright garish colours others fading, for several hundred yards on both sides. Russell pulled the car in a side lane before the bridge and was lucky to get a parking space. They got out of the car, put their hoods on and approached the bridge on foot. Walking along the footpaths, they saw signs of life, paraphernalia of desperate existence right in the middle of the city. The rain was coming down hard, and puddles of water began to appear everywhere. The city lights were coming on, and passing cars were splashing water on the pavements. There were cardboard boxes strewn on the ground, few shelters haphazardly made from cardboards with rags on roof and sides; along the walls of the arches there were few tents here and there. The place was dimly lit with street lamps as the main source of light which was barely reaching under the bridge. A soul- destroying sadness pervaded the whole place, where hope is gasping for breath; avoiding the gaze of city dwellers and hiding in shame. The evening rush hour was underway, cars passing in both directions splashing rainwater on the sides.

Their wipers making 'whooshing noises', their occupants utterly oblivious of the plight of their fellow citizens just yards away from them.

The 'unfortunate ones' who just could not keep pace with them, left behind in the mad rush of life, progress; the collateral damage of our obsession with materialism and belief in state sponsored' care only. The 'departments and professionals' not family, friends and neighbours.

As Emma and Russell made their way to the right side of the bridge which appear to be more 'populated', an Afro-Caribbean man was sitting on a wooden crate covered with rags wearing an old worn jacket, his dog was sleeping beside him.

Russell approached him cautiously.

"Hi, we are looking for a man, a friend and an ex-army man," he said hurriedly as if expecting to be waived away.

"Have you seen him? his name is Damien."

"No sir, I did not see nobody," the man said baring all his teeth.

Another man was sleeping on his side on some cardboard boxes spread out on the ground and some empty cans and bottle around him. Emma gestured to Russell not to approach him.

Another man strolled towards them, and Russell repeated his question. The man was comparatively better dressed and appeared helpful.

"Hi, I am Sam," He shook hands with Emma and Russell.

"We know some of the guys by name, but not all, he declared. On this side, nobody 'moved in'." He said 'moved in' with as much clarity and emphasis as used anywhere else where a new occupant would move into a house or apartment block.

"I would come with ya." He stepped ahead of them, and Emma and Russell felt somewhat safer. He asked another man sitting in the makeover home built with cardboard boxes and few rags and perhaps some wooden sticks.

Sam repeated the description of Damien but forgot his name.

"His name is Damien, Emma interjected. He is an ex-army man, his leg is artificial" stopping to realise the absurdity of her description in a place where people are in a mental and psychological torpor to neglect themselves to the point of harm, they are unlikely to notice a man with an artificial leg who once served in the army.

Sam took them to the entire right side of the bridge area and declared with certainty "not here."

"You should try the other side, pointing to the sparse south side.

"I'll come with ya," Sam said. He seemed to enjoy the trust placed in him by Emma and Russell in this briefest of human interaction.

"Many thanks, you are so kind," Emma said in gratitude. He turned towards the couple and gave a nodding smile. They walked to the other side, Sam leading them. Russell had switched his torch on which he used intermittently as not to startle anyone.

The first man, no, this can't be him. He was sleeping on his back but had a cap on his face; he too had a dog beside him.

He did not look like Damien and Damien did not have a dog. They moved ahead, Emma spotted another man lying on his side, his back towards them. A blanket was partially covering him, and he had a brown checked shirt. Emma stepped ahead of Sam and Russell in anticipation.

"Damien is that you!" she shouted. The man moved a little and turned towards Emma. "Damien, I have been searching for you, you should have called me."

Sam felt happy and satisfied, he smiled with a wide grin, "that's great man, you found your friend."

Russell shook his hand and thanked him.

CHAPTER 27

Damien's eyes were closed, he was shivering and shaking, and Emma could sense he was in delirium, possibly with high temperature; his colour was ashen grey and forehead sweaty.

"Russell, call the ambulance" Emma was hysterical.

Russell dialled 999. The operator asked the usual questions, is patient breathing? Is he conscious? Level of emergency response, is the patient infective? Anyone travelling with him? And so on.

"I think we need to take him to hospital urgently, he is in bad shape," Russell pleaded with ambulance people.

Emma was still talking to Damien with his head in her lap.

"The address?" call handler asked Russell,

"Where are we picking him up from?"

"We are under a bridge in Graysford, a railway bridge and several people sleep rough here". He sounded helpless, as if ambulance may not come for a man with no address. Russell thought of as many landmarks as he could remember as he drove to the place.

"There is a BP petrol station on the left just before the bridge and a Kwik Fit garage before this. Sorry, I don't know this place." Russell offered his apologies.

Ambulance call handler appears to have some idea of the place. Russell gave her his mobile phone number just in case. "Don't worry, we'll try to get there as soon as possible, response time is not guaranteed, are you staying with the patient?"

"Yes, we are." Russell hung up thanking the call handler. He lit up his torch again and noted that Damien was in a terrible condition. His lips were bluish, he appeared clammy, lips were dry and cracking, and his eyes were frequently rolling up, he was mumbling something from time to time but too slow for Russell to understand. Emma had shown him a picture of Damien before, and he was not expecting to him see like this.

Emma still had Damien's head in her lap and was comforting him. Russell was fearing the worst and wait for an ambulance for each passing minute was unbearable.

"Ambulance may take twenty-five minutes, or perhaps longer, it's not guaranteed. Damien looks very ill, and I think we should take him to our car and drive to the nearest hospital." Russell said in desperation

Emma nodded and shook her head.

It took a lot of effort for Russell and Emma to pick up Damien as he appeared floppy, clammy and very ill. Emma held his leg as Russell picked him with both his arm under his back and supporting his head with other. They stumbled out of the darkness, avoiding the obstacles and rubbish on the ground towards the arch, where they could see some light coming through from the street. The rain was falling in sheets and all they could see the relentless march of vehicles in both directions as it was past six now. The silhouettes of three people would light up briefly with headlights of the passing cars with ominous dark arches of the bridge in the background.

Emma heard screeching siren and the flashing blue lights of an ambulance as cars were splitting in both directions to allow it to pass.

Emma desperately waved to the ambulance crew who had spotted the three of them and pulled the ambulance on the footpath in front of the large arch. The blue lights of the ambulance were casting an eerie splash of lights on the old, dilapidated bridge and its forlorn surroundings.

The smartly dressed paramedics, one of them a woman jumped out of their vehicle. The paramedic quickly got a stretcher trolley from the back and then taken hold of Damien from Russell, who was tiring out now. They were all drenched in the pouring rain. The woman paramedic placed an oxygen mask over Damien's head, while the other crewman asked Emma some questions about Damien, his condition before, his medical history that sort of things. The trolley was pushed inside the ambulance, and a blanket was wrapped around Damien to keep him warm. His colour looked a touch better, but his eyes were still closed, and he was shivering and cowering to one side. The paramedic made the final check for their journey to hospital.

Emma stepped forward and asked her where they will be taking him to.

"Royal London Hospital," She said and slammed the door of the ambulance and shortly after its engine started and the ambulance pulled on to the main road, blue lights flashing and siren blaring as it sped away through the evening traffic. Emma and Russell were huddled together in the pouring rain, saw it move away and slowly walked to their car.

Russell could see Emma was badly shaken with this ordeal; he put his arm around her to comfort her. They got home at about nine and were utterly exhausted.

～つ

Emma and Russell woke up late the next morning. They both slept like weary travellers who have been through a burning hot desert and have found some shade for now but well aware what lies ahead.

They have to check on Damien's condition. Emma phoned the hospital to enquire. She was told he is still in intensive care unit, and his condition is critical.

"We need to go to the hospital and speak to the staff, doctors." Emma looked worried.

"Fine, that's right." Russell got out of bed.

They got to the hospital about noon and made their way to ICU. Emma checked with reception and asked if she could speak to doctors caring for Damien.

"If you could take a seat in the waiting area, I will pass your message on, and somebody will be with you shortly." receptionist informed her.

Emma and Russell waited, no words exchanged between them, each lost in their own thoughts, as different thoughts passed through their minds. Events of last night, Damien's desperate condition and where he was found were so sad and depressing. Russell had not met Damien before and to find an ex-army veteran, who fought for his country, in such circumstances in the middle of city with his eyes sunken, face pale, shivering body curled up and lying in squalour had a profound effect on him. His thoughts wandered to Pam, how she would be; she too had an important hospital appointment coming up after undergoing scans and tests.

Emma's mind was clouded and not able to think straight, to see Damien disintegrate so fast was heart-breaking for her. But why didn't he contact her? she would have come to see him, prevented his eviction, paid his dues or found an alternate accommodation for him. Perhaps his pride came in the way, or he just wanted to step aside as she was getting back together with Russell after so many months or may be both.

It appeared to Emma that Damien did not want to disturb her at this time. Did he make the ultimate sacrifice? He wished Emma all the luck in the world, though he was grateful for her presence, her love and support for him, he had indicated so many times that Emma should not be wasting her life after him. Emma was so full of guilt as the focus shifted to her meeting with Russell, to exchange their life stories, that was not easy for her either. Perhaps that was the time Damien was left alone, and maybe this made him slip through the only safety net, Emma, he had in this world. If she had been checking him every other day at least, he would not come to this state. She was now on the brink of losing a friend, through her own neglect; the guilt was wearing her down.

They have been sat waiting for forty- five minutes, and still, there was no news and no contact. Hospital waiting areas have an atmosphere of their own, and this was no ordinary waiting area but right outside an ICU. Everyone present here has someone critically ill inside hanging with their fingernails to life, thankful to all the technology, medical expertise, care and attention of the ICU staff to keep their loved ones alive and return to them safe and sound. Time seems to stand still here. People hardly talk to each, avoiding each other's gaze wrestling with their own thoughts which lurch from hope to despair to compromise.

Both Emma and Russell had never been to such a place in their life, their wait as agonising as everyone else. Finally, they saw an ICU doctor come towards them, his name written on his green theatre tunic. He asked them to follow him to a quiet room and sat them down. He asked him if they are family. "He has no family members contactable at present; his parents are deceased, and he was the only child, we are friends," Emma explained.

"Unfortunately, he is not in good condition, he has pneumonia affecting both his lungs. The infection has spread to his bloodstream called septicaemia. This is causing harm to his organ systems especially his kidneys and brain, there is some swelling on his brain, and that's why he drifts into clouding of consciousness, this should improve as brain swelling gradually goes down. We have to keep him in ICU until he is stable," the doctor explained.

"Is he able to talk? Can I see him?" "Yes, but only briefly," come with me.

Emma stood up and looked at Russell, who gestured her to go. She followed the consultant. He opened the big door of ICU and Emma had her first glimpse of what is it like to fight for your life. There was a vast bay with glistening floor with several beds, perhaps eight. There was medical apparatus, pipes monitors, more wires attachments and pipes and stands with drips, there were ICU nurses, staff, doctors, all dressed in same green dress as soldiers of an army. Among this paraphernalia of medical technology and personnel, actual humans were lying in various slumped positions connected to multiple pipes, wires, attachments and monitors. A nurse stepped forward and took Emma's hand and took her to the last bay.

This was Damien.

Unmistakably Damien! but not what Emma remembers of him and almost unrecognisable from his photos in the army uniform standing in front of an armoured Jackal vehicle.

Damien, the second lieutenant in Royal Scots Dragon Guards, was here in ICU attached to modern medical technology and apparatus and fighting another battle. He had an oxygen mask on.

Emma could see the intravenous drips and several wires and attachment from his body to the various monitors on three sides of the beds. He was in hospital dress, and his top buttons were all undone for wires and attachments.

His eyes were closed; the nurse stepped forward and put her hand on his shoulder, and called softly, "Damien".

Emma stepped forward to lean next to the nurse.

"Look, Damien. Someone to see you here," She removed his mask, Damien opened his eyes. Nurse moved and made way for Emma to come closer.

"Damien," she held his hand, "this is Emma."

Damien looked at her, "Thanks for coming, Emma" his voice low and crackling.

"How are you, Damien, you will be fine." tears now welling up in her eyes which she did not want Damien to notice.

He pressed his hand and Emma could feel his grip. I am fine; just want to rest for a while longer, perhaps very tired. Emma felt as if a dagger has been put through her heart the way he said those words.

"You should have called me Damien." Emma now broke down in tears, she could not hold herself back any longer.

"Thanks, Emma, you had done enough for me already, I will be forever grateful for that, don't forget this. The time, love and affection you gave me means a lot to me, now and hereafter. I may or may not see you, do take care of yourself." His voice was wavering and the effort of talking made his oxygen level drop. The nurse stepped forward quickly and put his mask back again.

"You will be fine, I will see you out of this place, sound and healthy I'm sure of this." Emma held back her tears and summoned all her conviction, all her courage to smile.

"Goodbye for now, dear."

"Goodbye."

Emma could see his lips mumble only. She pressed his hand and turned and followed the nurse and looked back only once as she reached the door.

She came rushing back to the waiting area and fell in Russell's arms sobbing. He patted on her back to comfort her.

～○

They were back in her flat and slept until evening as Emma's phone rang.

She sat up; it was a call from the hospital. Damien has lost his battle for life. His condition had deteriorated after 4 pm, he was put on a ventilator, doctors did all they could but could not save him, the receptionist told her.

Russell also sat up, looking at Emma; he knew where the call was from. No words exchanged, Emma clung to Russell crying and sobbing.

CHAPTER 28

Russell woke up at 10 am and was still wanted to lie down a bit more. They were mourning the loss of Damien and were utterly exhausted. His phone rang, and his mother was on the line.

"Russell, I am sorry to wake you up, dear."

"There is a letter for you, arrived here yesterday, I called you, but perhaps you were busy."

Russell's thoughts immediately turned to the events of yesterday; he did not want to alarm his mother. Yes, I was very busy, one of the friends was taken ill badly; both me and Emma were in hospital till late at night. He did not give her the news of Damien's death, there was no point.

He immediately knew this would be from Pam, but she could have called me, he thought.

"The letter looks personal with address written in longhand and no return address at the back, can I redirect this to you where you are." Russell had told his mum about coming to stay at Emma's apartment.

"Yes mum," He gave her the address slowly so that she gets the address right and requested her to drop this in the mail today.

"I will, dear."

"Take care, mum, I will be in touch soon."

～

The letter arrived the next day. Russell noted Pam's neat handwriting on the envelope redirected to him.

He opened it carefully; it was indeed from Pam, on her *'Florarama'* letterhead, this read;

> *22/09 2005*
> *My dearest Russell*
>
> *I hope this letter finds you well. I did not want to alarm you, but I thought you would want to know especially if something happens to me.*
>
> *I went to see the cardiologist at University Hospital, yesterday and the news is not good. I have got severe narrowing of the valve of the main artery, called 'aortic stenosis.*
>
> *I must have developed this over some time, and doctors reckon this is the cause of my symptoms of shortness of breath on exertion in the last six weeks. They have marked me for an operation to replace the heart valve, a big operation indeed.*

Cardiologist was quite upfront and straight about the risks involved, and this frightened me; without operation, it will only get worse. This cannot be cured by medicines.

I did not want to alarm my son, Peter, so far away. It is not easy to contact him as he is working offshore on an oil platform in Angola. The earliest he would get any letter from me would be in two weeks.

I did not wish to burden you for making a decision for me at this time of your life and being away from here. After much thought and soul searching, I have said yes, and my operation is planned for coming Tuesday at the university hospital under Dr Benson.

My sister, Lucy, will come from York and will go to the hospital with me and stay with me after discharge. This is very kind of her, and I am so grateful to her.

I know how much you love and care for me and would have come here straight away, but I did not want this. You need to be where you are at present with Emma, and I am happy with this.

The time spent with you in the last few months was the best period of my life, howsoever brief, and I will always cherish that. I am going to be in very capable hands, and I don't want you to worry too much over my operation and recovery.

In all probability, the operation will be a success, and I will be back in my little den 'Florarama' very soon. I would love to see you there once more.

I, sincerely hope that your reunion with Emma is a happy one and wish the best for both of you. If this happens, do promise me that you will bring her to meet me one day in 'Florarama' and in my home. Give my love and best wishes to her.

There is a small chance that I may not return from this operation. Doctors have quoted a chance of 3% whatever that means. I want you to be strong, look forward in life, taking all the positive energy from the time we spent together and not dwell in the past too much. I have lived my life, and there are no regrets, and above all, I met you.

With you, I found that pure unconditional love which people yearn for all their lives. If I am not here, this thought will comfort you, I want to see you happy and fulfilled in life.

With all my love
Yours Pam
X X X X

Russell sat down and slumped in the sofa, letter still in his hand, tears welled up in his eyes. He checked the date and postmark on the envelope, it was posted three days after it was written and three days in transit to reach him and today is Wednesday, that means her operation was yesterday.

This thought gave Russell comfort that she will be back in the wards after her operation. All sorts of images flashed before her eyes. He could not imagine seeing her in a hospital gown on a bed. Hopefully, she would be fine, these operations are fairly routine these days, he reasoned.

He read the letter, again and again, it was written in her usual style, open and optimistic, but there was a sense of foreboding he could not shrug off. She will be fine, so many people undergo this type of operation, and she was otherwise a healthy person.

Why did she write all those things? as if writing her last letter, the doubts raised their heads again.

Emma was waking up now and saw him in this pensive mood with a letter in his hand.

He showed her the letter, Emma was deeply moved, and Russell could see her eyes were wet and misty.

"Don't worry, she will be fine." She said in a low voice. Damien's shocking death was raw in her mind, and she was grieving the loss of a friend.

Russell called the university hospital, and after nearly half-hour of trying, he reached the ward where she 'could' possibly be recovering after her operation.

He spoke to the receptionist and gave the full name of Pam and asked her if she could give him some information on her condition and when will he be able to talk to her.

Receptionist was unable to give him any information even after asking many questions about him but promised to pass his message to her immediate relative, her sister Lucy. Russell provided his mobile phone number.

After an agonising wait of thirty minutes, he got a call from Lucy.

"Russell, I am Pam's sister Lucy. I am very sorry to inform you that Pam has passed away. She died during her operation." She was sobbing uncontrollably. "I was waiting for her, she never returned from the operation theatre. She asked me specifically to pass any news about her to you. Sorry, I could not phone you earlier, I was so shocked."

"What! how can this happen?". Russell was numb, and he slumped on the sofa, his call disconnected. Probably this was the reason receptionist was not giving him any information.

Emma came running towards him and saw his face covered with both hands, she feared the worse. Emma hugged Russell tightly, he broke down in tears.

"She has gone," tears streaming down on his cheeks, "just like that, she was here one day and now no more."

"Life is so cruel," he continued to wail and sob in Emma's arms.

After Damien's tragic death only two days ago, another terrible blow, at least she saw and carried Damien to the ambulance, Russell did not get a chance to say goodbye to her. Emma had not seen Pam but could tell from Russell's description of her that she was someone special. They sobbed in each other's arm; their grief was shared. In the space of two days, they have lost people who shaped their lives, given them something to live for and touched them in a way no one else could.

Russell was inconsolable, this lightning bolt has sucked the life out of him; he was barely able to pull through this dark time with Emma's support. She had shown great resolve and dignity to absorb not only Damien's loss but Russell's grief over Pam's death.

CHAPTER 29

Russell felt numb, just numb. It was shocking to the core of his existence. He felt his will to live is just ebbing away from him. It was only a few weeks ago she met her for the last time, she appeared fresh as her roses in *'Florarama'* and now this. In life and in her death, she chose not to worry or burden anyone.

Paradoxically Russell felt relieved, she chose the moment to leave while still happy, free from any burden of a disabling disease, she took flight from this mortal world. He could not envisage her getting old, needing medicines every day to stay alive, her face wrinkled and needing help for her everyday chores. This was not Pam's world, and she managed to live among all of us in this chaotic world, full of problems at her own serene pace in her own *'cool sequestered vale'*. She could not have lived without *'Florarama'* a retired existence. She chose to retire from life and the world in just one stroke.

Russell's bereavement would not follow a classic well-described pattern. This was something different. He would feel soul-destroying sadness one moment then rationalisation, denial, anger, bargaining and finally acceptance doing a wild dance, jostling for positions in his clouded mind.

Emma could feel his pain, she was herself going through bereavement after the loss of Damien, at times they would both reminisce about the departed souls and the impact they had on their lives. Their grief seems to have fused and have become one, each could feel this, but no one wished to put this in any formal words, and there was no need. Perhaps going through bereavement at the same time made them feel for each other more, they could feel the grief, rationalise it and accept it as time wore on. At least Emma had a chance to see Damien, she saw him in a terrible state, almost moribund, she could touch him, take him to hospital. Russell did not get this chance; she saw her happy and well in her usual jovial mood on their last meeting, and she simply did not come back from a routine operation.

Russell thought long and hard, who is to blame, there must be some mistake, an operator error perhaps. These operations happen all the time, why she? "Everything happens for a reason", Pam's voice resonated in his head and then some relief followed by another cycle of dark desolation. Emma was the best companion; he would not have coped with this grief tearing at his heart without her, and she needed Russell as much through this difficult time.

Emma suggested Russell should attend Pam's funeral. At first, he refused but then thought long and hard and agreed.

Russell was in touch with Lucy, Pam's sister, who was with her in her last days when she came for her operation. He expressed his desire to attend Pam's funeral with Emma. Lucy shared so many traits of her sister, she was aware of Russell's intense devotion to her and their deep bond of friendship. Pam spoke so fondly of Russell. She agreed and passed all the information about her funeral service, people attending the ceremony in St Stephen's Church and the whole order of funeral service. Lucy described the details of service, commendation and farewell, funeral procession and internment in an email to Russell. She told Russell; Pam's son Peter will be attending the funeral. She also reserved a place for Emma and Russell in her car for the procession.

Russell expressed his wish to put a letter and some flowers in her coffin which Lucy gladly agreed. Russell and Emma drove north to Russell's apartment in Duxford. It was a sombre moment, a sad day, they hardly talked during the car journey. The weather was cloudy, wet and miserable. Pam once asked Russell to bring Emma to see her, and he was just doing that but only with different time and space, different parameters, life is so fragile.

As Russell looked back on his companionship with Pam especially when he went to see her at her home and she consoled him to find his own social moorings and extracted promises from him to see Emma with open arms. Looking back, this all seemed to fit in as if she could foretell the future, as if she knew what is coming and what lies ahead. She knew somehow that their companionship in this world is a brief one and perhaps she made sure in her life to guide Russell to his destination. In doing so, she enriched his life with this enduring power of love which will last him a lifetime

All her words, all her musings rang so true now that she has gone.

On the day of the funeral, he drove with Emma to Pam's home to pay their last respects and joined funeral procession to St Stephen's Church with Lucy. He was dressed in a black suit and a bow tie, Emma had a long black skirt, a matching top and a black hat, she wore black pumps.

It was an overcast day; the church was filled with mourners. Pam's shiny wooden coffin was surrounded with bouquets of flowers and candles. Russell brought her favourite flowers, a bouquet of light purple lilies and dark purple Cala lilies and placed them by the side of the coffin.

He felt composed and felt some solace deep down. Pam's journey with him was to end here, but in few 'brief 'moments, she touched his soul, supported him through the utter lows of separation and gave him hope. She was like a beacon which showed him the ways to love, forgive even rationalise; when her work was done, she was gone.

The raindrops were clattering against the tall stained-glass window behind the altar, and it got darker outside. The minister read from the book of prayers as smell of fresh flowers wafted across the church. It was a small tribute to a life well-lived; Russell felt better. He left his message in a letter tucked in her coffin, 'souls can communicate', he thought and reasoned.

He specially wrote a translated verse of poetry in his personal letter to Pam, which is to go down with her.

> *With darkness all around me,*
> *She always lit a candle*
> *Her companionship was measured in months,*
> *in this mortal world*
> *It was a journey of centuries in my heart*

The funeral service was over; the coffin was carried by pallbearers to the hearse for committal service and burial. Russell and Emma joined the cortège as Lucy drove them in her car. As Pam's coffin was being lowered into the grave, Russell stood at the edge and put her favourite flowers in the grave. He then threw some earth into the grave with other mourners around the grave. The autumn leaves were rustling and falling to the ground around them.

"Rest in eternal peace! Pam, will see you in heaven." he mumbled. He turned back towards Emma, who was waiting for him. Emma wiped her tears; she noted Russell's eyes were misted.

CHAPTER 30

Russell and Emma had been back for two weeks now and began to make sense of changes to their lives. Fate had put them on a path they never thought they would ever take. It was on this road they met the two angles of mercy, or you may call them just good humans who stole a few months from their lives to stay on this earth for a little longer; for one last act of kindness.

Emma had contacted Damien's colleagues in Royal Scots Dragoon Guards. They had received his ashes and informed Emma about his last rites.

Damien's ashes were interred at Aldershot military cemetery with full military honours. Emma and Russell had attended the service for internment of his ashes. The ceremony was sombre but dignified. This brought some closure for Emma, who felt at peace. She remembered an oriental poet's verses she read some time ago.

> *What is life?*
> *Merely appearance of order*
> *and symmetry in elements*
> *what is death?*
> *just disintegration of these elements*

Damien's ashes, his 'stardust', his 'elements' were returned to earth, to the universe; an eternal cycle of life.

It was the second week of November, the autumn was here, and leaves were changing colours to brown, beige, orange crimson and yellow.

Russell loved this time of year, the rustle of falling leaves and changing panorama always fascinated him. Just a reminder of the cycle of life, meaning the end of one season that everything will lie dormant until next year and then spring to life with a fresh beginning.

"Autumn colours and scenes are my favourite; they are so calming. We will go to Tiverton Lake this weekend will have the same chalet booked for us." Emma shook her head. "That will be so nice; I want to be close to nature for a while, away from here."

Saturday 12 November 2005 was a crisp, clear day. There was a feel of winter in the air, days were shortening, and nights were longer. There was a thin layer of frost on the cars in the morning.

Emma and Russell drove to Tiverton Lake. Russell had his canoe 'Tempest' tied to the roof rack securely, they have a couple of bags. It was a one-hour journey. They checked into their wooden one-bed chalet, set their things up for the weekend and drove to the southern end of the lake.

Russell unpacked and unloaded his canoe. He did the usual checks and adjusted his pedals. Emma got in first then Russell and he started to row. It was early in the morning, and there was no wind.

The lake was just a mirror with tall pine birch and willows in majestic fall colours; a tapestry of orange, red, yellow, ochre beige and greens reflecting into the calm waters of this enchanting lake. There were not many people about, and the calm of the lake was only broken by the sounds of the pedals striking the water and 'Tempest' just just leaving a long trail of turbulence on the surface of lake. Emma took a deep breath and looked around as she admired the sheer majesty of the scene.

"It's so peaceful, so pretty", she said with a smile. "Indeed, it is." Russell began to peddle the canoe with steady strokes.

～

ABOUT THE AUTHOR

Shahid Zuberi is a doctor by profession and is also an accomplished artist and keen photographer. 'Shades of Endearment' is his first novel. He lives in the Highlands of Scotland and draws his creative inspiration from the beautiful landscape of Scotland. His paintings are regularly exhibited on major art websites and are held in private collections around the world.

He studied at University of Warwick, England and Royal College of Paediatrics and Child Health, London. 'Shades of Endearment' is set in 2005 in Britain and explores the multiple and often unspoken dimensions of love and endearment. It is a story of immense charm, emotional intensity and the incredible power of love.

Printed in the United States
By Bookmasters